FAREWELL MY ZOMBIE

Also by Frankford Publishing:

NOISY ALIEN COMMUNICATOR

FAREWELL MY ZOMBIE

Short Stories About The Undead

by:

Jackrabbit

Matt Bitonti

Derek Davis

Ev I.L. Frazier

Bertram Montiekowicz

Paradox Pollack

Isaac Helmsworth

Frankford Publishing
PHILADELPHIA

FAREWELL MY ZOMBIE

Short Stories About The Undead

Frankford Publishing Number 2 — Grayscale Edition

This is a work of fiction. All of the characters, organizations and events portrayed in this collection of short stories are either products of the authors' imaginations or used fictitiously. Any resemblance to actual events or places or persons, living, dead or undead, is entirely coincidental.

ISBN: 979-8-9872146-4-0 (Trade Paperback)
Library of Congress Control Number: 2025900379

Cover Image by ArthurPopular*
Cover Design by Shellerville

Illustrations by Samuel Burbury Hanchett
instagram.com/samuelburbury/

Additional Illustrations by Ty Thomas
instagram.com/amstudios11/

For Kelly

Contents

Illustration by Ty Thomas

FAREWELL MY ZOMBIE

by Jackrabbit

LOOKING OUT THE WINDOW, to see if there is any activity outside. Dirty and unshaven, his hair is so crusty it looks like he's taken time at the end of the world to add Murry's pomade to his coiffure. And his clothes smell.

Her voice lilts across the room to him. "Baby?" Too loud, his inner critic worries. "Kevin, is something wrong?" He can hear the anxiety in the question.

She wants him to come to her. She wants to be intimate. She wants to be touched.

"No, Sugarpop," he says in a loud whisper, "I'm just looking out for us." Now he's getting anxious. He doesn't want to run the risk they're close enough to the house to hear Monica and him talking. It's too dark to feel like he'll see them coming if they are out there..

Where they stopped for the night feels vulnerable to him. But she likes it here. She likes the nice house by the woods and the water. She told him she'd always dreamt about a nice house by the water as a kid. Was he going to argue with her childhood dream? There wasn't anything he wasn't ready to give to her and he knows it.

"Baby, come on over here. I need to talk to you about Yellowstone."

He doesn't like the idea of leaving the window, but he likes the idea of talking back and forth across the room even less. He leaves the moonlight and walks towards the candle by the couch where she sits.

"Yellowstone?"

"Was that a scoff?" She smiles, "You're scoffing at me? You think it's crazy of me to want to talk about a network TV series at a time like this?"

The candle on the coffee table didn't seem like a good idea to him, but she insisted. It sits there next to the shotgun. The light from the candle dusts them both with a wan orange glow. He sits down next to her.

"No," he says with a grin, "I don't scoff. I'm not a scoffer." He reaches out to hold her hand as it rests on her knee. "What was it? What were you thinking?"

"Just that we remind me of Rip and Beth, except you're not a heartless killer and I'm not a psycho."

"Hm," he strokes his chin as he looks up to the ceiling, "that sounds like it would make a great Valentine's Day card."

"Yes," she raises her eyebrows, "I steal all my best lines from Hallmark cards."

She tenses up suddenly, "Oh shit." she says looking over his shoulder.

"Ohmygodwhatisit?" He turns his head to see what she's looking at. Then in one smooth movement she sticks her finger in her mouth, covers it in spit, leans over to him, and then jams the wet finger into his ear.

He jumps as if he'd put his finger in an electric socket. "Oh my God, you goofball!" He says smiling as he takes the opportunity to pull her closer.

She staccato giggles, revealing the gap between her front teeth; she's self-conscious about it, but he finds it irresistible. "You're rethinking coming up to me at that party, aren't you?"

"No," he says. He caresses her cheek with sweet gentleness and a light laugh from his chest. "It's a good thing, we got to party the night before the world ended. You know, I would never come up to start talking to a stranger, but my heart started getting all twisted up when I first saw you."

She asks, "Um... did you think you might be having a myocardial infarction?" She laughs at her joke.

"No. Did you think I was a creeper?"

She giggles some more and pulls his hands to her breast, "No. We were at a drag queen dance party. I thought you were gay."

He brings her hand up to his lips to kiss her fingers.

A look of disgust takes over her face, "I have not been able to shower since this whole thing started. You think I smell, don't you?" she asks.

"Ah, no. I don't smell it, baby. I grew up on the street. Things like that didn't bother me before the world was an apocalyptic hellscape." He caresses her hair. "You're beautiful, I love you."

They kiss.

The smell of her fills his sinuses and he loves it. A musky rich scent; he's sure he must smell at least as ripe.

Their lips come together with a supple resistance. Enough firmness to assert desire for more, but yielding enough to say, I want to feel you, to be present with you here. Now.

He reaches under her shirt. His warm calloused hand sends a shiver through her; moist anticipation blooming. He squeezes her. Flexing the muscles of his arms, she feels surrounded by gentle iron bars. A reflexive moan escapes her throat as her head swims with lust.

He freezes.

"What's up, baby?" She says with a frown.

"I heard something." he whispers.

Flushed with arousal—her emotions raw and exposed—she pouts. "Yeah, that was me getting turned on."

"No, no." He looks away from her with furrowed eyebrows.

They haven't had sex since he found her sheltering at her job. There hadn't been time to put on makeup. She was feeling dirty and unattractive. Was this sudden distraction his way of blowing her off? Did he realize he'd made a mistake in coming to look for her?

"Are you trying to be cute?" She frowned at him, "You know I'm the cute one."

"No, I think I heard something."

Now the magic of the moment is gone and she's frustrated. "You're just saying that because you don't want to have sex." She puts her hands on his chest and pushes herself up so that she's straddling him. "You don't think I'm pretty."

"Aw, baby, please don't say things like that. I'm just really anxious about—."

A figure leaps over the couch and tackles Monica onto the floor. She screams. Kevin jumps up off the couch, grabbing for the figure as it wrestles with the struggling woman.

Charged with adrenaline, Kevin rips the writhing body off of Monica. Unburdened, she brings a leg between her and her attacker, kicking up with everything she has.

The momentum of the kick sends Kevin and the squirming mass tumbling away across the room.

He scrambles to his feet—bringing his hands up, prepared to fight. But the candle has gone out and the darkness disorients him. There's not enough light from the window for him to...

The room explodes in a flash of light and sound. For a fraction of a fraction of a second he sees the thing's mouth inches away from his neck before the violence of the shotgun blast sends it flying into the wall.

"Fuck, how did you see anything?"

"I couldn't," is her terse response in the dark.

With urgency Kevin finds his backpack leaning up against the wall where he left it. Digging through it, he finds his flashlight. Gathering himself he joins a silent Monica who is hovering close to the moaning creature.

"You said you think they just don't feel pain?" She asks as they watch the thing die within the circle glow he shines on it. It looks to have been an unremarkable middle aged woman. Black blood shines as it pours out of the massive hole in its midsection.

"That's what I figure." He shrugs. "No pain."

"I wanted to watch you love each other," the creature wheezes, "but I was too hungry." With a barely audible whistle, it expires.

"Oh my God, that was so sad." Monica can't tell if she is horrified and disgusted or overwhelmed with pity for the poor thing.

"We got lucky. That felt way easier than it should have been."

He turns to her and shines the flashlight on her, "are you ok? Did you get scratched or bit? Let me see?"

"I'm ok." She holds out her arms to show there's no marks there. "How about you?"

"Honestly, I feel like Jules from Pulp Fiction. I have no idea how it is I'm not on the floor with that thing."

"Yeah, sorry about that," she says—handing him the still-smoking shotgun.

"It's cool, baby. You saved both of us. How the hell did it get in?"

She shrugged. "When we got here we climbed in through the window and checked the doors to make sure they were all locked. I don't know... maybe she had the key?"

He looked up at her with a frown.

"That is one more thing we figured out about the virus," he sighed, "It ruins your respect for people's privacy."

"There's no way it's safe to stay here," she notes.

"Well, the way I figure it is that if there was a pod of them they would have attacked us all at once. My guess is that she was here for the same reason we are—isolation." he caresses her arm, but she pulls away.

"I'm worried that one of them may have heard the shot." Concern tightening her voice.

"Me too. But, I wouldn't feel any better running around in the dark." She nodded agreement, tentative but acquiescing as he continued. "You have to figure that unless there was one of them right nearby anyone that heard the shot would have to find their way through the woods." He put his hand on her shoulder. "I'll take the first shift. Why don't you try and get some rest." He kisses her forehead and turns to illuminate the corpse cooling on the floor. "I'll move this thing outside."

She's sitting at a table.

She notices it's the table where, as a little girl, she sat for years eating dinner with her family back in Gary. There's a metallic odor coming from the food on the plate in front of her. It's the rose China her mother saved for holidays. There is a feeling of nostalgia that washes over her. A sadness at what is lost and can never be recovered. Memories of her dog, long dead and buried. Her mother's laughter at Christmas. This rush of longing increases in intensity so fast it shocks her as if she's been caught in the waters of a flash flood. It isn't desire that beats in her ears with a relentless urgency, it is need screaming up from the depths of her reptile brain. Intense. Primal. Irresistible. Reflexively, she grabs at the food on the plate and jams it into her mouth. Then she shoves the plate between her teeth and bites down so hard it shatters. She claws the table cloth into the endless pit of her mouth and then breaks the table apart into sticks and splinters she can't consume fast enough.

Wide-eyed and gasping she sits up on the couch. She didn't think she'd be able to sleep. It would have been better if she hadn't. She didn't feel rested at all.

Still panting from the jolt of waking from the nightmare, she looks around to find herself alone. It's her, the shotgun, and the streak of dried blood leading out the door.

Fear of abandonment chuckles by her ear. Her heart empties as gooseflesh crawls up her back.

He left her. She's alone with nothing.

Footsteps on the stairs. "They're coming for me," she thinks.

Launching herself from the couch, she snatches the shotgun from where it leans against the wall. Spinning around, she levels the gun at the empty doorway; finger poised at the trigger.

Walking through the door, Kevin jumps at the sight of the gun barrel staring him down.

From behind the gun she asks, "Are you ok?"

"Baby. I'll be better once you stop pointing that gun at me," he smiles with his hands in the air, "I'm fine, thanks for asking. Happy to report that it was a very boring morning. I scouted the area and it looks like we're in the clear."

She frowns disapprovingly before she points the gun to the floor.

Putting his hands down he makes a weak attempt at humor, "I thought you'd be happy to see me."

"You left me," she says with a mixture of dejection and resentment.

"You were sleeping and I didn't want to wake you up. I'm sorry that I scared you." He comes over to kiss her but she turns away as he comes close.

Sensing he's crossed a line he was unaware existed, Kevin adopts a more penitent demeanor, "Fine. Look, I said I'm sorry. I won't leave you again without letting you know where I'm going, ok?"

"No. No, it's not ok." She frowns, "How can I trust that you're not going to just leave me?"

Kevin's eyebrows raise and his back straightens. "Of course I'm not going to leave you. I love you. I fought my way across a city filled with flesh eating zombies to find you."

"That's what you say, but you don't even really know me. What if you decide that I'm not the girl you thought I was?"

"Sugar, I love the person that you are," he emphasizes the last word, extending his arms out in a pleading gesture. Opening himself up to her; leaving himself vulnerable to her.

"You don't think I'm attractive," she mutters.

"What?" Kevin's jaw goes slack at this, "Of course I think you're attractive! You're a babe. Why would you say something like that?"

"You haven't had sex with me since you tracked me down." She turns away from him and crosses the room to the window facing the front yard.

Kevin puts both hands behind his head, hugging his temples with his forearms. "We've been running for our lives! There has barely been time for us to kiss."

"See!" Whipping around to face him, anger polluting her face, "You don't even respect my feelings. I told you I'm feeling abandoned and you won't even acknowledge me."

At this Kevin slumps down into the couch.

     FAREWELL MY ZOMBIE

He looks at his hands. "I guess I thought that we shared something special when we met. I'm sorry, if I was wrong."

"I didn't need you to save me, Kevin!" She says his name as if she was his teacher, shaming him for getting suspended from school. "I was doing fine before you showed up. I'm not your friend." At the end of this sentence she narrows her eyes and leans slightly forward.

He feels himself shaking. It distracts him. That's good, he doesn't want to feel how terrible it is to have her yelling at him. His body doesn't feel like his own. His breath comes in an unfamiliar rhythm.

Kevin looks up in despair with a deep frown and pleading eyes. "Baby, I'm sorry."

It'd been crazy for him to trek across a ruined city to look for a girl he'd known for a night before the world ended. He knew it was crazy, but he did it anyway and when he found her and she was happy to see him, it seemed like it was meant to happen.

Finding love when society was coming apart at the seams made the worst of times seem alright.

Now it actually did feel like his world was ending.

"I am so sorry," he stutters, "I didn't mean to scare you. Maybe you just need a minute to yourself?"

"See!? This is exactly what I was just saying. You were just going to leave me. You were always just going to leave me. Just get out!"

He starts to protest, but she interrupts him. "No! I don't want to hear it, you're a toxic asshole. Just leave."

"Ok," he says quietly as he stands up from the couch. He's defeated. This is harder than any challenge he had trying to reach her. He fought zombies, now he feels dead inside.

"You should hold onto the shotgun." He says to her without looking up. Moving slowly, he picks up his pack. Now he looks up at her and says, "Whatever happens, I really think you should join us at the warehouse. It's not so far from here."

She returns his offer with a cold stare.

Shoulders slumped, head hanging, he shuffles through the doorway.

She stands staring at the doorway—still as a statue—for what feels to her like a very long time. Her breathing starts to become more shallow and quickens. A single tear issues from her left eye cooling her cheek as it rolls down to hang at her jawline.

She takes a sudden gulp of air and throws herself onto the couch head in hands quietly sobbing.

After a time her breathing slows and the tears dry on her cheeks.

With slow hesitation, Monica reaches a shaking hand beneath her mane of thick black hair to the back of her neck. Holding her finger in front of her face she sees the blood from the wound at the base of her skull. The wound from when she was bit last night.

Kevin is the sweetest man she's ever known. She didn't feel like she deserved him. She hates herself for pushing him away, but there wasn't any possible world where she was ok with him seeing her turn into one of those monsters.

She looks past her finger to the coffee table. Where the shotgun sits. Waiting.

A gasp leaps from her chest as she fully accepts that she's been infected.

She reaches for the shotgun.

Outside the house Kevin stops to lean against a tree trunk. He is unable to believe that this is actually happening. He starts to weep quietly.

He knows this is bad form. He's leaving himself vulnerable, making himself a target if there are any hostiles nearby. But, there's no stopping the rush of sorrow that's overtaken him.

It was too much to ask for, too much to hope for, but what is life for if not love? He loved her and that he would be there for her no matter what she thought.

Shaking his head, he realizes that she was wrong.

She thought that he wasn't going to show up for her. He made the mistake of thinking she was right. But, his commitment to her was rock solid. She was saying what she said to him based on a false assumption.

She was wrong in thinking that he was going to leave her. He'd be there no matter what. He was going to be there for her. If that was what she wanted. And it was what she wanted. He knew it was.

His heart broke to hear her say those things. She thought he was letting her down but that was the last thing he wanted. Something he'd never do.

Still leaning against the tree, he straightened up with resolve. He was going to just clear things up. He was going to just make sure that she knew that, as far as he was concerned, he was going to be committed to her for as long as she wanted him to be. And if she still wanted him to leave then he would. But, he needed to know that she knew that he was all in.

Determined, Kevin wipes the tears from his face and starts to retrace his path.

That is when he hears the shotgun blast coming back from the house.

A rush of adrenaline sets his teeth on edge. That's not good, he thinks. That's bad. Shotgun fired is bad.

He sets off to run, then to sprint and he's through the open door taking the stairs two and three at a time. He wants to scream out her name, but he can't risk bringing any more attention to their location.

Through the door he sees the body on the ground. He's frozen with horror, then staggering forward into the room, he stares down at the bloody heap.

"I'm feeling a little neglected here."

Startled, Kevin looks up from his horrified reverie to see Monica standing across the room—the shotgun slung by her waist, a wry smile on her lips as if she'd just eaten a canary. "Oh my God!" He pants, "I heard the shot, what happened?"

She sighs, not quite exasperated. "I was just sitting here," she pauses for a moment. "Thinking—and I heard someone coming up the steps. I thought it was you coming back to me."

"Shit, I'm so sorry! Did I not shut the door? I must not have closed the door when I left." He grabs his head in his hands as he looks around the room. "I can't believe I did that."

"It's ok, I'm glad you actually did come back," she says. Looking down at the floor she mutters, "I'm sorry. I'm sorry that I didn't tell you what was really eating at me."

"What do you mean? What didn't you tell me?" His anxiety rises. His ears get hot.

"It's just really hard to say this. It's scary. I don't want to have to admit it. I want to pretend that things are fine. That I'm fine. That there is a normal for me to go back to."

"What is going on?" He asks while reaching out to her, getting closer.

She pulls away.

"I got bit."

     FAREWELL MY ZOMBIE

Hot ears ring. The world feels like it is shrinking around him. It's a pressure from every angle. He's at the bottom of the sea.

It can't be. This isn't happening, he tells himself. "No! No. It can't be." He pleads with her.

"It happened last night. The thing got a in a bite on the back of my neck. You couldn't see it. It's under my hair. I don't have much time. I'm already starting to feel sick. You should go."

He sets his face in a frown. "No, I'm not leaving you. I should never have walked out that door without you and I'm not leaving you now."

She shakes her head. "I love you for that, and this is so scary. But, you have to go. I am so scared. I don't want you to leave, but I don't want to hurt you. Please just go."

"Listen to me. I don't care. I don't want to leave you. I'm here for you. You're saying that I should worry that you're going to turn into a monster and eat me? How likely is it that I get eaten if I'm walking out there alone? And even if I turned I would still want to be with you. Whatever that hunger is that drives them crazy," he steps towards her and lifts his hand to her cheek, "That's how I already feel about you."

For a moment she closes her eyes and tilts into the hand resting on her cheek. And then she pulls away shaking her head 'no'.

"You're the person I always wanted. I didn't think you existed. I never felt like I deserved someone like you. And I can't have you." The tears drip down her face and fall to the floor where they mix with the black blood congealing at their feet.

"You're worth it, baby. Of course you're worth it."

He's floating weightless down a tunnel. There's images projected onto the tunnel. The images are of the room and him and Monica. He hears his voice. It is saying, "Just let me hold you."

He is crying as he wraps his arms around her. "Maybe they'll come up with a cure," he says into her hair. "Miracles happen, right?"

She sobs quietly into his chest before pushing him away.

Gathering a resolve she wishes she didn't have, she shakes her head and pushes the shotgun into his hands. "Just go, baby. It's done."

"Go!" She doesn't yell but the intensity comes through her gritted teeth. "I don't want to eat you, ok? Go."

Crestfallen, he takes the weapon from her and stumbles back so that he's being supported by the door jam—legs unsteady beneath him.

"Farewell, my zombie." he says into his chest as he turns to walk away.

CALIFORNIA SOBER

by Matt Bitonti

IT'S NUCLEAR HOT OUTSIDE, and this robotaxi has no
air conditioning. It doesn't matter. The target can't hide from me.
I'm jetlagged from my journey, so the car and I slowly ease around
LAX airport. The Little Tree air freshener rocks back and forth.
Royal Pine. We swoop like hawks gliding the warm thermals. At
least the music is relaxing: Claude Debussy's Clair De Lune. 91.5
KUSC on your FM dial.

My name is Vobert, or Vob for short. And I'm a long way from
home, 25 light years or thereabouts. What am I doing on Earth?
Sitting and sweating in bumper-to-bumper traffic, nauseous, like
everyone else. I pass by a bleak rental car parking lot guarded by
spike strips. I've been to Earth a hundred times and still can't believe
tourists pay to come here.

The driverless car keeps circling. The wheel keeps grinding. The
yellow sun shines over the concrete desert, and the Earth turns. I
sigh. I've only been gone a day and a half, but I already miss the
blue-white tinge of Vega's starlight. This golden sun's overbearance is

exhausting. Such is the life of an regional inspector. Someone needs to protect the consumer.

Then, outside Terminal 7, I spot him: a corpulent figure, bald, wearing expensive sunglasses. A wobble in the man's gait gives him away—another Vegan. But not the way you're thinking. He's from Vega 9, like me.

I mash the "pullover" button on the armrest, and the taxi tries to comply. But it's all taking too long. The target eases himself into a void black Mercedes Maybach.

So I eject myself out of the car. I keep a traffic cone with me for this very purpose and put it in front of the taxi, halting its logic. It will stay like that forever, or at least a few hours until a tech happens by.

I half float and half hover my way toward the chauffered car. I move with the uncanny agility of an alien wedged into a human costume, one who doesn't care who notices. With all the conspiracy theories, no one would believe it anyway.

I arrive at the car just before it pulls away. I tap my knuckles on the window, and the passenger inside freezes. Life pauses, and I feel his tremendous internal debate. He's evaluating the stakes of running and the effort of the chase. My eyes convey a ragged tenacity. You're not getting away. And he knows this because he finally lowers the window.

"Are you Vark of Vark's Interstellar Tours?" I asked.

The fat man nods, and I flash my badge. The light blue gemstone swirls, and the ornate metalwork gleams. The artifact can only be Vegan. His mouth gapes open slightly.

"My name is Vobert, and I'm your regional inspector. I need you to come with me."

Vark understands the gravity of the situation. He can tell how far I've come to check on his burgeoning business. He knows the punitive measures I can take. There won't be a trial. Home is 25

          CALIFORNIA SOBER

light years away. With these inspections, I'm the judge, jury, and executioner. But hopefully, it won't come to that.

Wordlessly, Vark climbs out of his fancy car and dismisses his driver. We bob and weave back to my generic taxi, still hapless. "Get in the front," I say. I watch Vark do as I command, then remove the traffic cone. The cone and I sit behind him, a move I learned from the Earth movie "The Godfather." For a bunch of primitives, humans certainly have a flair for the dramatic.

The taxi resets, and I instruct it to drive to Beverly Hills. I assume whatever scheme Vark is up to will be near money. We pull away. Vark, the car, and myself. A family sitting silent. He's calm. I'll give him that much.

Then he glances nervously over his shoulder at me. "Hello, Carlo," I want to say, but hold back. That would make me Clemenza. I'm on official business with the full authority of the Vegan government. And it's all recorded—no time for quirky movie references.

"We've been watching you for some time, Vark. Quite an operation you have running here."

We sit at the blinking red light near the 405 North on-ramp. Two a time for carnage. It's as good a place for an inquisition as any.

"Please," he begs, "I can explain."

"Oh, you'll get your chance. But first, you're going to answer a few questions." We zipper merge, and Vark nods in silence.

"What would you say you do here on Earth, Vark?"

He clears his throat. "Don't you know?"

"Of course, I know." And I do. "I just want you to explain it in your own words."

"Mr. Vobert, was it?"

"Just Vob is fine." Formalities won't help him at this stage, only the truth.

Illustration by Samuel Burbury Hanchett

"Well, Vob, I run a small business." He pauses, pulls out a handkerchief, and wipes his forehead. The white car roasts in the midday sun and Vark's nervousness only adds to the heat.

"Go on."

"I help travelers from Vega 9 settle here on Earth."

"Travelers, huh? According to their families back home, you're scamming the elderly."

He denies with his whole body, shaking his head so hard that the cabin tilts back and forth. But I bring out a notepad and continue.

"There have been multiple accounts of citizens liquidating their assets, taking to the wormholes, and living out their lives on Earth, never returning. Do you deny this?"

"I have many satisfied clients. Most don't go back. But that's because they love it here! No funny business."

Vark isn't lying. A dozen sensors confirm this. And even further, I can tell from his mannerisms and his specific vocal range. He is running a legitimate business, or at least has lied to himself so convincingly that he believes it. But still, it's all so implausible.

"Okay then, Vark. You say a Vegan would purposely sell everything they own and bring a suitcase full of gold and jewels through a wormhole so that you can guide them around Earth? This backwater dirtpile? Given all the other options? Prove it."

He flinches. "Right now?"

"Don't test my patience." I try not to think of my brood at home and what they would be doing now. "Take me along on one of your normal days. I must experience what makes Vark's Interstellar Tours such a successful organization. The type where hardworking Vegans come to this little dust mote and never return home. They must be pretty great, your tours."

"They are." He sighs, still reticent. "Fine. But to be clear: I'm not breaking any laws on Vega 9."

"Sure." He purposely says nothing about Earth's laws.

"So, you're not in touch with the local authorities, are you?"

I scoff. This investigation is getting interesting. "I represent the interests of our home planetary system. Nothing more."

"Okay." He sits back in his seat, resigned. "I just flew in from San Francisco to meet two new clients. You can watch it all go down." He then gives the taxi a new destination: Venice Beach. We transfer to the 10 and creep the last few blocks after the exit. Vark has the air of a salesman, compelled to make small talk, but every time he starts to say something, he stops, remembering everything he says can and will be used against him. By me.

We park a half block from the boardwalk, and the taxi charges my account. I take the traffic cone and wonder when these things get cleaned. Probably never. I look up the history of the traffic cone. Of course, it was invented in Los Angeles.

The salt air smells fresh. At least that's something. I start to wonder if Vark is stalling. I'm watching the garish yellow sun bounce off the Pacific Ocean when I see two more Vegans, obviously a couple, emerging from a T-shirt shop. Mirrored sunglasses. One's wearing a black tank top with "King" in a script font. He's also got red shorts with an arrow instructing to "Pull down in case of emergency." The other is the "Queen," apparently.

The salesman puts on his best smile. "Well, if it isn't the Vabbershams! It's so great to meet you in person, finally. I hope your trip was easy. Welcome to Earth, I'm Vark," he says, sending a meaty palm toward his clients. "And this is my associate, Vob." He tilts his head in my direction. "Don't mind him. He's just a trainee, shadowing."

I'm too seasoned to be offended by the battlefield demotion, but I can't help but note how lying comes easily to Vark.

"Hi, I'm Vandell," says the larger one, "and this is Venitta." Handshakes all around, and the usual small talk. Is it your first time on Earth? Oh yes. How was your trip? Long. Are you excited to be here?

The Vabbershams hand over a rolling suitcase full of valuables. Vark pays the T-shirt mongers 1800 dollars for custom tank top outfits that look to be worth about eight dollars in total. In case you're wondering how a beachfront one-star vape juice kiosk survives in one of the highest rent districts on the planet.

"What a deal," exclaims Vark. "You both look fantastic!" And they believe him, as they don't have any context to make them think otherwise. "Come, let's walk. Are you hungry?" They nod. "Of course you are. Let's eat."

We shamble northwest toward the Speedway and take a left onto Pacific. Vark sidesteps the street buskers and waves his arms through clouds of vape smoke. He walks backward, leading us tour-guide style. His steps have a practice—a routine, not just for my benefit. Good. If Vark can remain this honest, he'll make it through the day alive. It's my job, but take no joy in destruction.

"What makes this planet so interesting, particularly this region, is how welcoming the locals are to aliens from Vega. Look, for example, just over there."

Sure enough, a sign in a store window proclaims in block letters: "Immigrants and Refugees are Welcome Here!" I am curious to know what kind of refugees can afford 900-dollar imported handbags, present company excluded. But not curious enough to stop to investigate.

We turn right onto Rose Street. "And look over there," he points to a sign in a restaurant proclaiming they are "Vegan Friendly." The Vabbershams smile and nod.

"What does it mean to be Vegan Friendly, one might ask. And it's a fair question. These humans, a subset especially popular in this region of California and Nevada, identify with our home planet. They worship us! So much so that they live a clean lifestyle, free of pesticides, antibiotics, and other pollutants. They eat food derived only from fruit and vegetables but don't sacrifice for taste! On the contrary, the food here is unparalleled in quality."

Vandell grunts. "The hibernation process has left us practically starving!"

"Don't worry, because right now," Vark continues, "we're going to the culinary epicenter of Veganism. I promise you it's the best Vegan cuisine around. And you'll be... grateful that you made the effort."

Vark's awkward joke becomes apparent as we round the corner to 5th Avenue to see a restaurant: the Gratitude Cafe. It's weekend brunch, and there's a line out front.

But Vark didn't get to where he is in this galaxy by sweating the line. He sidles up to a host named "MK" and slips them a hundred-dollar bill as he's motioning toward our hopelessly touristy-looking group. Miraculously, a table is ready.

They walk us to a booth in the back. "Have you ever been to Gratitude?" MK asks us as they hand out menus. "He has," I reply, "but we haven't."

"Well, welcome back to our veteran," they say, nodding toward Vark. "And to our newbies, please know that the point of Gratitude Cafe is to serve only the cleanest ingredients, designed to amplify intentions and achieve peak flow." We aliens sit. Talking wouldn't be appropriate, like interrupting a religious ceremony, so we don't.

"Enjoy the divine bliss," MK says as they leave the table. "Your server will be with you shortly."

"See what I mean," Vark giddily remarks, and the Vabbershams laugh.

"Is that person ours?" Venitta asks. And for a second, I think she forgot a word. Then it dawns on me. I see now what kind of business Vark is running: we're on a hunt.

Vark shakes his head nervously. "No, that's not your server," he blurts. "Your... meal will be provided by someone else."

I note the passive voice. It always shows up when circumstances are about to get diabolical.

"Go on, Vark, don't mind me," I say. "I'm just a lowly trainee, after all."

He looks like he's about to panic, but deep down, I know he's found a loophole. It's nefarious. But nothing he's doing is against the laws of Vega 9. "Why don't you show these nice people who will provide their meal."

Vark looks over at the bar. "There," he purses his lips in a kissing motion. "The bartender."

Everyone at the table looks over at the bar, where a tan and somewhat disheveled man wearing a T-shirt that says "I WANT TO-FU" looks up from a blender. He notices Vark and smiles, giving him one index finger. Even an alien like me recognizes the universal meaning: I'll be over in a moment.

"Friend of yours?" I ask Vark.

"His name is Jessie," Vark says, his voice drawn thin. "But everyone calls him Slim."

The irony is apparent, as he's not skinny at all, quite the opposite. By the time Slim comes by, the Vabbershams are practically drooling. "Hey Vark, my main man! You're not in my section, but you know that wouldn't stop me from saying hi."

"Oh, I know that wouldn't stop you, Jessie." Vark gives him a tip for no reason.

"Wow thanks. Namaste. But call me Slim, dude. Remember? Slim-shady, you know, whatever's clever." Everyone at the table laughs hard. But it's not that funny. Vark stands and gives the bartender the world's most awkward bro hug. "These are my friends from back home. They're Vegans, too."

"Right on, man, right friggin' on. Well, you guys look hungry, so try the breakfast burrito. It's unreal, like the size of my head. I don't know how they get that vegan queso so creamy! Well, I do know, but I can't tell you, or I'd have to kill you!"

Another not-so hilarious joke. Oh, Slim. If you only knew.

"So listen, Slim, before you go, can you tell my friends what you told me the other day? About the plague of being human?"

"Oh, what, how I'm a part of the worst invasive species on the planet? Don't get me started. Humans love damaging the planet through multiple means, man. We start wars with each other over bullshit human constructs. We're unnecessarily brutal to animals when we don't need to be. There's so much violence, starvation, exploitation, and brainwashing. Our compassion extends nowhere near the amount of harm we've done. Any act of human good is a drop in the bucket compared to reversing the pain we inflicted on everything else. We don't benefit this planet. We're a plague."

The Vabbershams smile and nod politely. "Thanks, Slim," I say, against my better judgment.

Vark orders for the table, then we wait. Seventeen minutes later we politely shove a few ounces of human food into our costumes. The creation is spicy, delicious even. I smell the cumin and the saffron. But this food won't satisfy the hunger of a real Vegan from Vega 9. Not even close.

Vark shoots a meaningful look at me and stands up. "Well, I will arrange for your actual meal: the finest in genuine Earth cuisine. Then we have to go, you know, busy, busy, busy."

Vark walks over to Slim/Jessie, and I overhear their conversation. Long story short, Jessie agrees to act sick, take the rest of his shift off, and show the Vabbershams the underside of the Santa Monica pier for the bargain price of two thousand American dollars. I look over at Vandell and Venitta, their sunglasses unable to hide their giddy excitement.

Vark arranges the bill and puts the leftovers in biodegradable to-go trays. With a smile, we leave the Vabbershams behind. Vark pulls the roller bag, its plastic handle sagging heavy with pirate treasure.

"One more stop," Vark says. "Will you order one of those robotaxis?"

I do as he asks. Under my breath, I hiss. "So, you know what they are going to do to him? Right?"

"You heard him talk. He's a plague upon the planet. Practically sacrificial. And I think he's still a virgin."

"And what about the police?" Surely, Vark's scheme draws attention.

"Half of the murders in this country go unsolved," Vark notes. "Half. But it won't be any murder without a body. He'll go missing. Maybe someone will presume him missing or declare him dead. Or not. No one cares. Life is cheap. We're in the wilderness."

"It's an audacious business model," I remark out loud. Vark waves his hands.

"Don't worry. The locals even have a name for clients like the Vabbershams: Zombies."

A quick search of the term through the wi-fi, and I'm dumbfounded, which doesn't happen often in this job.

Vark sees an unhoused gentleman near the corner and gives him the leftover breakfast. "You wouldn't happen to be a Vegan, sir, would you?"

The homeless man is more cagey than Jessie. Almost anyone sentient would be. But especially someone living on the street. Still, he opens up after seeing Benjamin Franklin on light green paper. Yes, he hangs out by Gratitude to eat the Vegan garbage. "Just because I live like this doesn't mean I deserve less."

Indeed. Vark flashes (fake) studio identification and takes a few pictures. "These are the before's." He gives the man another thousand dollars with the promise of a makeover. The man looks from side to side for any other conceivable option. But he has nothing left to lose.

Eating the cumin-saffron burrito leftovers, the man climbs into another robotaxi. I grab my traffic cone from the curb. Vark announces the addresses. First, a hair salon in Santa Monica. Then, over the hill to Calabasas.

This whole situation is ridiculous, I think to myself. I should cite Vark for a dozen major violations and go home.

But then I feel my digestive glands activate. My teeth itch—the real ones, under the human suit. Theoretically speaking, the razor-sharp teeth of a Vegan would glide through any human's bones. I imagine a whole basket full, breaded and fried. Like crispy french fries. Salt, maybe some honey mustard. It won't travel well. The fresher, the better.

Vark splashes his cash again. Despite not having an appointment, we watch the man in the hair salon getting shampooed. Vark stands with me outside and tells me about the next stop.

"These clients, they aren't like the Vabbershams. More high-end, more generational wealth. Sleek. They wear black. They take less risks. They have lived here, like, forever. But they only emerge at night. Theirs is a... liquid diet."

I lean on the robotaxi, perplexed and frozen by my trusty traffic cone. I look through the window at the man, already looking more like a tanned businessman than a vagrant.

"And he's your container of liquid."

"Vampires. That's us too." Another V word, the trademark of any good Vegan. I search the term, and again, cannot believe the lore that's been built around it. Vark or someone like him has been running this scheme for centuries. Maybe longer.

I lean against the robotaxi door and sigh. With a casual swipe of my human costume's hand, I bumble, and, what do you know, I accidentally turn off the camera.

"What if, and I'm just throwing this out there, I don't cite you for any violations today." Vark's eyebrows curve inward with relief.

"But there's a condition."

He's desperate, hands together, begging for mercy. "Anything, anything you want, Mister Vobert."

"Find the Vampires another liquid container."

An evil grin from Vark. "Of course. You wouldn't be much of a regional inspector if you didn't sample the goods."

Illustration by Samuel Burbury Hanchett

ALREADY DEAD

by Matt Bitonti

THE GROUND IS WET, but Taggs doesn't feel it. He slumps against a pile of sandbags, a dirty blanket about his shoulders. His breath hangs in the winter air. Everything's just above freezing, himself included. It smells like burnt toast. He coughs and drools a little. The medic leans in and shouts a question at him.

"What's your name? Do you know your name?"

His full name is Tommasino Angelo Tagglieri. That's the name on his birth certificate. There won't be a death certificate. Society collapsed a few months prior, taking paperwork and bureaucracy along with it.

He'll answer to Tommy. But everyone calls him Taggs. And that's what he croaks out. "Taaaggggggssss."

The medic nods, confirming the patient still has his wits about him.

In the before-times, he played football. A nose tackle at the local college, muscular and squat. But no one plays games anymore.

The medic cracks the smelling salt packet and puts it under Taggs' nose. The downed man starts and winces. But it works. The ammonia smell pulls him back. He's on the bench, on the sidelines. He's back in the game.

His chest aches like he's taken a couple of sledgehammers to the ribs. But he's awake now, eyes wide, full of wonder and surprise.

"Look, Taggs, there's no easy way to put this," the medic says. "You were stone-cold dead."

Dead wrong. Dead right. Dead nuts accurate. So many idioms use the word. But a person doesn't want to think about what it means.

From the demeanor of the crowd huddled nearby, it must be true. Taggs feels like he's at his own funeral. Worse maybe. These people aren't mourning. They look at him with pity and contempt. The eyes never lie. The medic must have brought him back to life.

"Back off," one of the enforcers says. "Give him air." The medic talks words at him, and phrases like "acute cardiac arrest" and "advanced life support" fly over his head.

He sees the chrome paddles. Did someone yell "CLEAR" like in the movies? He hopes so. He stares more deeply at the paddles. In them, he sees the reflection of the low winter sky, purple clouds, and pale yellow beyond. Blackbirds sit on a dead power line, judging everyone. It's just after sunset.

Taggs swallows but that doesn't do much to wet his parched throat. He manages to ask, "How long was I out for?"

"At least six minutes," the medic replies. "You were passed out without a pulse when Selene found you."

Tommy looks around and finds her almost right away. She scrutinizes him with thinly veiled disgust.

Selene was a lawyer, a managing partner, no less, with an office on the 53rd floor. Now, she's the leader of the walled outpost they called New Hope. It's an impressive name for a shanty town of walls and tents crammed together on what used to be the property of the Philadelphia Water Department.

Why there? Well, in a word, water. A creek conveniently feeds the reservoir. There's also a field of solar panels and the technology to purify said water.

Sure, it's the high ground, already fenced in. But as society learns, over and over, clean water is everything. A man can go weeks without eating. Taggs could go more than that. But without water, it's all over. That's why they stay.

How did Selene force her way to the top of this improvised community? The same way many business fortunes were made in the before-times: by being the most sociopathic person in any room.

Taggs hears the undead horde scraping and keening on the other side of the gate. He usually doesn't notice. About a month after the zombies showed up, their groans faded into background noise.

With the chokepoints and the barbed wire maze wrapped around New Hope, it's hard to distinguish how many are out there. It could be a couple dozen, it could be hundreds. Ultimately, there are too many to count. And who even wants to? That's the thing about zombies. They are slower and dumber, but they always have the numbers.

For the first time in a long while, Taggs doesn't worry about the horde outside. He's more concerned about the gathering mob inside. He tries to stand and fails. If there were a ref here, they'd stop the fight. There are sympathetic eyes but just as many scowls. Selene glares and shakes her head. That isn't good.

Suddenly, Taggs wonders how others see him. That's usually not his concern. Taggs loves himself and always has. He carries that confidence through his life. He's funny and gives great hugs. The people around him smile more. But after the end of the world, what's a smile worth?

After football, Taggs became a cook, first at a diner and then at a bar. Over time, he mastered the art of frying chicken strips and dipping them in honey mustard. Too slow for the scavenger squad,

Taggs continued in that service role after zombies appeared. He's the food guy. Always has been.

What can he say? He loves meals, maybe a little too much, but he also appreciates helping people. It's his job to help feed the masses. It's his job to keep up the spirit inside the walls. It's simple work but necessary. At least, he always thought so before today.

Most days, he works at a makeshift tent assembly that acts as the social heart of the camp. People call it "the Pub." Taggs is again a short-order cook and pretty good at it, considering how much he improvises with meager ingredients. At one time or another, every citizen of New Hope has eaten a meal from him—even Selene.

And that's not all. During the day, he works with the farmers, lifting, hauling, and shoving. He does the brute labor the vertical plots require.

But let's be honest. How essential is Taggs to any operation? Other people can cook and tote sacks. Taggs has always been overweight, even before the zombies showed up. And being next to the food helped him stay that way. Having two jobs gave him access to double rations. Or, as Taggs thought of it, his usual amount.

For fun, he plays the guitar. After the kitchen closes, someone brings out the homemade sangria. Taggs plays with a three-piece band that calls themselves "Rough-house." They do 90's covers, and their singer prefers to rap in Spanish.

When Rough-house gets going, the zombies outside stop wailing. According to the guys on the guard towers, they stand still and sway in the breeze like grass on a windy day. They like Tom Petty and Sublime. "You Don't Know How it Feels" and "Santeria."

It's like the old saying: music soothes the savage beast. In those rare moments when the world is quiet except for Rough-house at the Pub, it is the best humanity has to offer.

Granted, he's humble. He knows he's not Dave Grohl. The entire world watched Grohl get ripped to pieces during the last Saturday Night Live.

Sitting on the ground, Taggs thinks, what do I remember last?

His last image is the sun setting through the growing beds. There's not much sun this time of year; it's mostly maintenance. He's on the afternoon shift, bending down to lug waste to the compost heap. Then, he staggers. A blinding pain runs up his shoulder, and he can't breathe. He crumples face-first to the ground—then, nothing—the enveloping darkness.

Taggs takes another look around the circle. The guys on the football team used to call him dumb. Prop 48 was one early nickname that didn't stick. It referred to the law about college athletes needing minimum grades to play. No one could believe Taggs ever passed anything. He's not book-smart, and he'll admit that.

But he's bright enough to see he isn't long for this world. Either he'll succumb to the heart problem that nearly killed him today, or Selene and the other leaders will vote him out of the group. It's obvious. Limited resources exist inside the walls, and they get more limited every day. The residents account for every scrap of food, energy, and freshwater. Everyone needs to pull their weight, and Taggs barely pulls his when healthy. As an unwell individual requiring recovery time, he's dead weight. There's another "dead" idiom: dead weight, dead meat, the dead of winter. And there's no tolerance for any kind of death inside the walls of New Hope.

They give him a day to recover before Selene convenes the show trial. He notices his food rations getting smaller and more pathetic in that time. Even the water the guards bring to his tent seems dirtier, somehow. It's rainwater, green with leaf particles. It's not the usual reverse osmosis stuff.

The next day, Taggs crams himself into his best shirt, a Jerome Brown Eagles throwback jersey. Everything's a throwback now. It's number 99, in white, double XL. It could be better. There are scuffs and a few holes in the polyester blend. Still, this jersey is his prized possession, even before the apocalypse, and he hopes it conveys his value to the judges assembled. Or at least his loyalty. It's his equivalent of a three-piece suit. Bringing it home for Jerome.

But it doesn't matter how put together he looks. The hearings are a facade.

Selene presents her case and she doesn't mince words. Her closing argument: "Taggs is greedy, gluttonous, lazy, and, should there be any future for the human race, unbreedable. He's a burden on the other citizens of New Hope, and while we all empathize with his health issues, there's not enough surplus for our society to provide a safety net."

Taggs gets his chance to defend himself and stands to do it. He groans like he's been in a car accident. He takes a breath and is about to launch his appeal to decency, to human kindness. But looking around, he sees what's coming. So he decides to go the other way.

"With all due respect to the council, I take great offense to these proceedings. Particularly the term, Unbreedable." Even though there's no one recording this trial, he still says, "Let the record show that many nights after the Pub, numerous citizens of New Hope found me very breedable." Laughter erupts. "Huggable, snuggleable, whatever you want to call it. On a cold night, I'm a space heater, like a furnace in your bed. Let the record show that Tommy Taggs, nose tackle number 99, is extremely breedable. The defense rests."

The small assembly chuckles. Taggs sits, satisfied. He can't change his fate, but he can at least choose the style in which he faces it. He wants to leave this world as he lived it, a crowd-pleaser.

The council members seated next to Selene don't need much time. It's a unanimous vote, 5-0 for Exile. The way things are outside the walls, no one survives long. Not unless they're heavily armed.

     ALREADY DEAD

For a guy like Taggs, it's a death sentence. Or, more accurately, an un-death sentence.

Taggs doesn't have much time to wonder what kind of zombie he will be. They are putting him outside at dawn.

His final meal inside is slightly better than in days past: Nutella, jelly, and crackers. Someone even smuggled in a fun-size Goldenberg's Peanut Chew for dessert. With the way things are, total collapse and whatnot, those little suckers are worth more than gold. What a worthless shiny metal that turned out to be. Taggs smiles. He still has some fans in this world.

He sleeps well, all things considered, and when he wakes, two burly bros from the security forces are leaning on his doorframe, ready to escort him outside.

"Stand down, fellas," he says with a grin. "I'll go quietly."

And he does, not resisting when they lead him through the maze. One of the guards, Donnie, holds him steady while the other unlocks the front gate.

Taggs and Donnie played ball in the before-times, both All-Catholic league. Donnie the guard and Taggs the nose waged wars against each other on the field. After school, Donnie delivered refrigerators for the big box stores. Taggs doesn't like to remember the world before but he can't help it. Chopping it up with Donnie at the corner bar. Donnie talking about entering one of those bare knuckle fights. He would have cleaned up. He has fists like honey roasted hams.

Taggs can tell by the look on his face he's wondering when Selene will push him out the gate too. All in the name of portion control.

"Don't worry about it, Donnie. We're all good. Always will be."

"It's a damn shame, Taggs," Donnie says. "The way this whole thing is going down. It friggin' stinks."

"Forget about it," Taggs says, patting Donnie on the shoulder. "Just remember, when you hear that guitar playing in the wind, I'm out there."

"You're a good man, Taggs. One of the last few." A lone tear rolls down Donnie's cheek, and he turns away. The other guard pushes Taggs outside into the morning fog.

The locks turn, and the guards retreat. It's quiet behind him, but ahead, through the mist, he hears the shambles.

What else can he do? Out of ideas, he walks to meet his fate.

He reaches the street corner. The six-sided street signs reflect the sunrise in green. He's on the corner of Queen Lane and Fox Street. There's a pile of cannons encased in concrete next to a big blue historical sign: "On this spot in 1777, George Washington rested his troops before the Battle of Brandywine."

It's as good a spot as any to make a last stand. He shivers. The fear creeps up his neck. He won't be playing any guitar in the wind. Why did he make such a promise? He'll be bit in minutes. Seconds. And then what? A groaning fungus on two legs? Maybe he wouldn't be self-aware. That would be a blessing.

He stands up straight. With wishful thinking and a brave face, Taggs is ready to die.

The figures approach, wearing pinstriped blue rags. They look like they used to work for the Water Department, and Taggs can even see a few IDs hanging around neck lanyards. These zombies are undead with all the time in the world, and all they want to do is clock in at work. Maybe it's muscle memory.

Shaking, Taggs closes his eyes and waits for a bite. But the pain never arrives. The zombies shamble past him and groan as they bang their heads against the cast iron gates.

He opens his eyes in disbelief. It's impossible they missed him. Taggs is too big to ignore. They just didn't recognize him as a target.

Taggs shakes his head and wanders toward the gas station. These zombies didn't want to eat him, but maybe others will.

He opens the door, hoping there's something left on the convenience store shelves. He never ate breakfast. So close to the settlement, it's probably wishful thinking.

It's dark inside and mostly trashed. It smells musty. A mouse scurries against the wall. The shelves are bare. But Taggs looks around, and underneath a toppled-over display, he finds an unopened package of Herr's Potato Chips. Long Hot's and Sharp Provolone flavor. Taggs' eyes light up. Even though it's expired, mostly broken pieces, chip fragments, he's overwhelmed with joy. If it's one thing he's learned post-apocalypse, expiration dates are a scam.

He doesn't even wait to get outside. Taggs opens the bag. Before the first greasy potato shard meets his mouth, he hears a voice.

"Unnnggg! PAY!"

A mustached zombie sits behind bulletproof glass in the corner, the logo for the gas station rotting off his polo shirt. Taggs can't believe his ears.

"Did you say something, buddy?"

"YOU PAY! Everyone pays. Or put back."

Taggs looks at the wall and sees a picture of this man in better days, his family posing in front of a sign. A foreign flag hangs, green and white. He wasn't just a cashier. He owned this place. Born on the other side of the world, he put all his life force into the gas station. And after he turned, there's nowhere he'd rather be.

Taggs stands and approaches the kiosk. "Sorry, boss," he says. "But I don't have any cash."

The convenience store owner slams a hand against the glass. "Caaaaard," he moans. "Use card."

Taggs smiles and spies a card on the floor. He brushes it off and presses it against the dead reader. There's no electricity, so he makes the noise.

"Beep!"

The zombie nods, and an earthworm falls from his rotting jaw. He thrashes his arms around and pushes a long scroll of thin paper through the slot.

"Thank you," the zombie says with the slightest of sing-songs. "Nice day."

Taggs walks out of the store, dumbfounded. Survivors have tried talking to the zombies. They showed no indication of speech or conscious thought.

But apparently, they do think. About going to work, and they talk when they get there.

Taggs eats his chips outside the gas station, and another group of zombies passes. Again, no response. Except for the last staggerer, who tips his dingy hat toward Taggs in greeting.

"Unngg. Go Birds."

Taggs stands there and says, "Go Birds," in reply. There's that muscle memory again.

It dawns on him. Zombies talk to other zombies. They don't converse with the living. Taggs stops chewing, and looks back at the cooking smoke rising from New Hope. He curses aloud.

The zombies think he's one of them. Because three days ago, he died.

For six minutes, the medic said. Would five minutes have been enough time? It's an engaging question, one that requires future experimentation. There's no one else outside the walls, though. No one alive, at least.

     ALREADY DEAD

A few minutes ago, Taggs was a dead man walking. Now, he laughs. He whoops and celebrates, even doing his trademark sack dance. He wiggles his knees and spikes his half bag of Herrs. He regrets that last move, but it doesn't matter. If the zombies accept him, if he doesn't have to fear their bite, that means the world, whatever's left of it, is at his disposal. He can do whatever he wants.

So, he does. First thing's first: shopping. These other zombies dress like they're going to work. Or whatever made them most proud in their life. So Taggs crosses the divided highway and enters an abandoned sporting goods store. The guns section is a ghost town, but he finds a taser stuffed under the shelves, new in box.

More importantly, he finds the football section and reclaims his past identity. He selects shoulder pads, a helmet, and his trademark, too much eye black under his left cheek. He thinks about adding the Jerome Brown jersey, but that's his formal wear. Too good for everyday zombie behavior.

Next, he turns deeper south into what used to be called a bad neighborhood. But they're all bad now. He hits the pawn shop. Inside, he grabs a guitar, an amp, hair clippers, and a wagon to haul it all. There's no owner here guarding the place. Best case, he's inside the walls of New Hope, fighting over half a bowl of stale cereal.

Taggs trudges up the hill toward the water plant. These houses aren't the nicest in town, but they're far from the worst. He picks the largest on the block, a corner property with a backyard garden and an array of solar panels on the roof. The inside is a mess, but miracle of miracles, the recessed lighting turns on when he flicks the switch.

"Gamechanger," he says aloud to no one. A few zombies wander close, perhaps drawn to the light. Taggs has only been a homeowner for five minutes but already feels territorial. He goes outside, ready to try out his new taser.

Zap. Plunk. He drops one, and it doesn't get up. The others don't react. They stare and continue to look at him dumbly. He takes out a second, then a third. Even goats and sheep would run away. But these zombies show no fear. They keep wandering over, and Taggs keeps putting them down. The almost invisible hum of the LED draws their curiosity.

At first, Taggs is amazed by his discovery. Why hasn't anyone thought of this before? It's so easy. But after about two dozen executions, Taggs gets bored, and his mind wanders. Maybe, he thinks, right now, there's a gang of cowboys in Texas, cattle prodding their way to victory across the grassy plains.

But he knows that's unlikely. It's not the miracle of electricity that makes what he's doing possible. Zombies can double-die in any number of ways. It's his immunity from having a near-death experience. That's the special sauce. There's no risk to this activity. They observe each other get popped. Then they watch him approaching to make them next. And they stand there. Maybe they want to be put out of their misery. It's just depressing.

He turns off the light, and whatever zombies he didn't get to scatter away. He drags the bodies into the street and plugs in his taser for what will no doubt be a busy day tomorrow.

He uses the last of the day's power on the hair clippers. Over the months, his hair has become ragged and clings to his neck. So, Taggs set the trimmers to number two. He hangs out the window, letting his trimmings fall into the garden.

Taggs checks his reflection: clean, intimidating, younger, even. He can still make out his hairline, and he's ready now. Ready for gameday.

The block is strangely quiet as he tucks into his sleeping bag that night. He considers his position.

"This all happened for a reason," he thinks. "I can help everyone." Taggs laughs aloud at the audacity of it all. It's like some comic book movie. Taggs: the unlikeliest of heroes.

      ALREADY DEAD

When, in the grand future, the people ask: who led this stand against history's greatest menace? Who saved us? The blue signs of the future will say, "On this spot, led by a short-order cook." No, he corrects his fantasy, "a great football player." There will be statues of his trademark shoulder pads, hospitals, and schools built in his name. Tommy Taggs Elementary.

The next day, Taggs wakes with the dawn and takes breakfast from this family's well-stocked pantry: kind bars and dried banana chips. He boils water and makes Earl Gray. How civilized. As he opens some Lorna Doones and dips them in the black tea, he reflects on how many unused troves like this are out there—probably tons. When the world ended, people lasted long enough to burn through their bullets but not nearly long enough to chew through their food supplies.

That was common knowledge back at the water plant. Selene even assembled scavenger teams, but when half the number didn't come back after every mission, Selene ruled that practice to be more of a special occasion, essential staples type of last resort activity. In New Hope, they don't risk turning everyone into zombies for tea.

After he eats his fill, he puts on his shoulder pads and gets to work. His coach used to say before games, "Just another day at the worksite, gentlemen. Get your hard hats and lunch pails."

So he grabs the taser, fully charged, and goes outside for another fifty or so easy "deactivations." He tosses the bodies over the concrete wall onto the train tracks. His mind wanders as he does his work. There are millions of zombies in this city alone. How many days of fifty does it take to get to a million? Taggs isn't one for Calculus, but he knows basic drug dealer retail math. After the morning haul, he marks it all out with chalk against a brick wall. Fifty taser hits a day, times 365, is 18,250 a year. Let's round that up to 20 large. It would take him 54 years to clear the rest of the city himself. And that's not counting the millions in the suburbs.

Illustration by Ty Thomas

It's funny. In the before times, our brains were comfortable with the idea of a million. A quarterback made a hundred million. Maybe two if he was a baller. Maybe some sap paid a million for this corner house with the solar panels on the roof and a small backyard pressed against the regional rail line. But a million isn't manageable by yourself. It's stupid big, a massive, soul-crushing number when you're tossing bodies over a wall.

Taggs feels that weight. He puts his hands on his hips and regards the sky. It's bluer and more transparent than any day he's lived through before. He takes a few deep breaths, closes his eyes, and hears birds chirping. They don't mind the bodies on the tracks. Neither do the feral cats.

So, big deal. Taggs needs help. He resolves to be there the next time someone gets shoved out of the gate at New Hope. But in the meantime, better up that zap number to a hundred a day.

He goes inside the house and recharges the taser. The house batteries are almost full, and he wishes this modern house had a DVD player. Then he wonders if living in the past like that would be depressing.

He walks down the street to the Free Library branch, intending to learn all he can about electricity. Storing it, using it, transporting it in batteries. His brother is a plumber. He was one, rather. Taggs doesn't want to think ill of the dead, but he was a dumbass who called electricity spicy water. Taggs' family understood pipes. How much harder could wires be? There's a lot of solar energy around these streets. If only he knew how to harness it.

It's dark inside the dusty building, the only light coming from a glass installation courtesy of the estate of Andrew Carnegie. After finding three or four books on the basics of being an electrician, Taggs walks toward the exit. But he doesn't see the figure leaning over the checkout desk, and it stirs when he gets close.

"Unnng!" The zombie says. "Check out." She's got glasses on a string attached to her head and a slightly askew wig.

Taggs stops at the barcode reader, but it's dead. Computers and the internet were some of the first things to go. But this librarian zombie isn't discouraged. She's got the ink pad and the stamp out, old school.

Taggs smiles and says, "Sure thing, hun." The zombie librarian doesn't have much motor control, but she manages to bash the stamper on the pad and then onto the books. She doesn't open the covers, and the last stamp hits him in the meaty part of his hand.

But it's no big deal. The world's over, and everyone left is on auto-pilot. Taggs can relate.

Books under his arm, he nods to the librarian and walks back toward his new house. Well, it's not new, but it's new to him.

He's startled by big round headlights heading his way. It's one of those rectangular blue trucks. Silent, an EV. It must have some access to fresh juice because it's as bright and quick as the day the corporation purchased it. There's probably another solar array where the vans are parked, and this zombie is just doing his job like any other day.

The van comes to a herky-jerky stop in front of a row house with a female zombie eagerly waiting on the porch. The deliveryman zombie puts on the hazards and grabs a dirty package from the van. He shuffles over to the front step and gives the box to the waiting woman. They each grunt in acknowledgment. Everyone's doing their job. Receiving packages from shopping must have been hers. He laughs as a funny word jumps into his head: Amazombies.

But as Taggs gets closer, he sees a dispute—or at least an impasse. The woman is trying to give back a different package.

"Bad shoes. NO FIT! You take back!"

"No," the delivery zombie states, "I only deliver. No return."

The receiver keeps trying to press the package into his hands, but the delivery zombie refuses. "UPS Store, QR Code," the delivery zombie keeps repeating.

Taggs stops in the middle of the two. "Thank you," he says, taking the package no one wants. "As it turns out, I work for the UPS Store. I'm the manager. Actually, I'm going there now. So allow me. Thanks so much, you're both doing great."

He moves to leave when the woman zombie grabs his arm. This is it, Taggs thinks; I've gotten too close, grown too cavalier, and they will eat me for dinner. But she doesn't bite him.

"Tracking number," she says. "What is tracking number?"

"Oh," Taggs says, his body sagging in relief. "Three. The tracking number is three. Go ahead and write that down. Have a nice day."

The zombies look at him dumbly as he nods his goodbye. Weirdly, he likes these two; how they interact reminds him of a simpler time. The thought comes, perhaps he'll taser them last.

But all that altruism goes away when he approaches his squatter house. Next door over, he sees a familiar figure forcing a refrigerator out of a broken-down doorframe. The zombie lacks the skills to remove door hinges, so he rips through the frame without regard. It's Donnie, the security guard, the offensive lineman, back to his lifestyle—big box deliveries.

The rotting smell hits Taggs before he gets close. He's turned. It's only been a couple of days? Was there an accident?

"Donnie," he says, "Donnie, put down the fridge and look at me. It's your boy, Taggs. Remember? From football? It's me, Tommy."

"Out of the way, Toppy." Donnie swipes at Taggs weakly. For whatever reason, Donnie remembers nothing except that he moves fridges.

Taggs isn't an angry man or one prone to revenge, but seeing his friend in this state stops him dead in his tracks. He knows what happened: Selene and the council members put Donnie outside for eating more than his share. It was easy to make an example out of Taggs. Then, they did what humans do naturally: follow precedent. Survival of the fittest, indeed.

Taggs goes inside and turns on his streetlight. Donnie and a few other zombies linger near the garage. He zaps about fifteen zombies he doesn't know.

Then, with tears in his eyes, Taggs hesitates before Donnie. He closes his eyes and sighs. He'd do it for me.

Afterward, fifty bodies pile up, a hundred. Then two hundred. But Taggs hasn't even scratched the surface of his anger. He breaks into every house on the block, looking for a firearm or some cache of explosives he can turn on New Hope. Of course, he finds neither.

But he does find energy drinks to fuel his mania. He keeps searching and zapping, day into night. He finds a trunk of Pennsylvania's best fireworks in the volunteer fire department's basement. It's a giant trove full of mortars, screamers, and firecrackers of all sizes. Looking at the pile, Taggs remembers the joy of setting off fireworks with his family. Barbeques and lemonade. The happiness he felt as a kid watching the colors dazzle against the summer sky.

Lost in the innocence of the past, the violence drains from his frame. The people who run New Hope deserve some retribution for what they did to Donnie and for what they did to him, too. But a different idea occurs to him. There may be another way.

Over the next few days, Taggs calls off his cleaning routine. Instead, he hauls the fireworks to his home by wagon. He reads his library books, experiments with launch tubes, and continues to scavenge.

He finds wires from the place that set up the billboards next to the highway. From the hospital, syringes, Narcan, and a fancy defibrillator machine are buried in an overturned ambulance. Those shiny metal pads that brought him back to life could do the same for another. If only he knew how it worked.

He dedicates himself to learning about electricity. It isn't easy, but he's got nothing but time on his hands. He laughs at himself when he realizes he doesn't need to know much to bring a portable charge up the hill, one big enough for his guitar amp, a microphone, and the various pyrotechnics.

The plan is simple. Just after sunset one night, Taggs will throw a big concert right out front of New Hope. They will be getting ready for bed, the night will be quiet, and they will be a captive audience. They will see what kind of life he lives outside. That will be his revenge. The best revenge is living well. His English teacher, Mr. Church, said that once. Well, he didn't invent the quote. It was quoting someone British, someone like Shakespeare, but the name escapes him.

Taggs doesn't know when it will happen, but he's waiting for the perfect night. And finally, a few cold weeks later, comes the darkness of a new moon. He hauls everything up the hill through the day, and he doesn't think the guards atop the tower are paying attention at all. He sets up a tent. He cracks a beer he's been keeping in a cooler full of ice. It wouldn't take much for them to realize he's not just another shambler. But they don't seem to be interested in what's happening outside. Taggs remembers that feeling. Just trying to ignore the world's ended. Take a nice long sleep and dream about how things used to be.

As the last slivers of daylight leak out of the sky, Taggs turns on the mic. "What's up, New Hope! Are you ready to rock?" No response from the walls.

So he takes a disposable Bic lighter, brown for good luck, and lights a fuse. A hiss, a whistle, and a giant bang above, purple flame splitting the night sky. It's one of those big rockets that Taggs should have shot high. But Taggs only got it up around three stories, and the explosion rocks the sky, spreading sparks over half the reservoir. Heads in the guard tower swivel in his direction. That woke everyone up.

Taggs starts strumming on his guitar. Then he launches into his set. It's his usual 90's covers. Tom Petty would be a great zombie, he thinks, just writing songs and smoking butts. He launches off a cluster of fireworks after every song. The zombies nearby sway and watch the sparkling sky with wonder. And Taggs can tell, everyone inside is watching, some even applauding from their spots near the walls. The guard tower throws a spotlight in his direction, and he thanks them.

"Good evening, thank you, please, you're too kind." Another firework display, again dangerously close. The cheers settle and he addresses the audience. "It's Taggs here, remember me? God, I've missed you all. Some of you, anyway."

There's an awkward silence and the mic whines with feedback. "You're probably wondering what's happening. How am I talking to you right now, playing songs, having a grand ole time with all these biters and shamblers right next to me?"

Taggs can feel the anticipation build. They are wondering that and more. "Well, what if I told you I have discovered a secret, ladies and gentlemen? And it's a big one. Big. Do you want to know my secret?"

"Screw you, fatass," someone says, in the sarcastic way people used to abuse each other out of love before the world ended.

"Well, fine, then, I won't tell you how I live out here, among the dead. I've figured out how to save everyone inside, maybe the whole world. But will I share it with you? Hell to the no!" Boos shower down, and Taggs waits for them to settle.

"And you know who's to blame for this? That council, which hoards all the best stuff. The ones that put Donnie out here to die. And me, too. They should be out here." Taggs pauses for drama. "Selene," he says, his lips pressed up against the microphone. The distortion makes him sound like a monster. Or God. "I'm talking to you, Selene. Search her tent," he says, "who knows what you'll find." He sighs. "And that's that. Until I see you out here, with me

          ALREADY DEAD

and my friends," Taggs waves toward the zombies, "I don't feel much like talking."

With that, Taggs packs up his guitar and retreats to his tent. The house is much more comfortable, but he wants to be nearby for whatever happens in the morning. He doesn't want another Donnie situation on his hands. The sleeping bag is warmer than he expects, and while he hears activity inside the walls, outside, by the hillside, the night is quiet. Still, he's having trouble settling down. The concert gave him a natural high. Taggs giggles a little before eventually passing out.

In the morning, he hears the sound of the gate opening and a distinctive female whimpering. She's begging. It has to be Selene, and the guards are shoving her outside.

"You don't get to treat me like this," she says. "I'm important!" There's no reply but the clang of the gate closing. She bangs on the door. Taggs emerges from his tent.

"Quiet," he says, "or you'll attract unwanted attention."

She sees Taggs, and her eyebrows furrow in rage. "This is your fault," she says. "With your concert and fireworks. You think you can help these people better than me?"

Taggs waits for her rant to wind down before replying but she's cut short quicker than he expects. A gang of Water Department zombies wander close and moan, baring their teeth.

"So, I assume you want my help?" He says.

She's petrified now. "What do you want, an apology? I'm sorry, okay? I'm just so unbelievably sorry."

He drops the first Water Department zombie. Plunk, zap, kapow, he takes down four more in quick succession. For a moment, it's silent, except for her ragged breaths.

"I don't need your fancy words," Taggs says. "I just wanted you to know how it feels."

"How?" She asks. "How did you know that I was hoarding supplies? An angry mob ransacked my tent last night."

"I didn't know," Taggs admits. "I just assumed. People like you always skim a little cream off the top."

"So what now," she says, "will you share your secret? There's more of them coming."

"I will help you, Selene, even though you never helped anyone. But there's a catch."

The moans of the undead gather closer. "Anything," Selene says. "I'll do anything not to get bit."

She sees him as a predator because that's how she sees the world. The strong and the weak, the controller and the controlled. But he waves his arms in reassurance. "Calm down," he says. "It's nothing as sordid as that."

"So," she says, "what's the catch?"

Taggs reaches into his coat and pulls out the defibrillator. He sets it down, turns it on, and it whines with full charge.

"The catch is, it's going to hurt. If you want to live, you're going to have to die first. At least for a few minutes."

He approaches her slowly, paddles first. "You should probably lie down first," he continues. "It's probably more comfortable that way. Although let's be honest, you won't like any of this. I know I didn't."

She shakes her head in protest. "You dummy, those machines don't work on active heartbeats. They have safety features."

"Oh I know," he says. "That's for the return trip."

He strikes fast, plunging a hidden syringe into her neck. The opioid acts quickly, sagging her frame. He watches her crumble to the ground, unable to speak. Then he prepares the Narcan.

A zombie crowd has gathered over Taggs' shoulder. He checks her pulse, which is slowing. The zombies chomp against the air, hungry, ready to bite, but as Selene's heart slows and eventually stops, they lose their appetite and turn their attention back to the gate.

Taggs stares at his watch. Six minutes. Is that too much? Would it work with three or four? It's better to be safe than sorry.

After exactly 360 seconds, he administers the Narcan and pops Selene in the chest. A real part of him doesn't want her to gasp back to life. But she does, coughing and crying. The zombies nearby don't even notice.

"Here," he says, handing her an open water bottle. "Drink this. Dying takes it out of you."

DESERT RAIN

by Matt Bitonti

ZOMBIES DON'T SCREAM. It's not like the movies. They're delicate, like a cat hissing. Or a snake sliding across the sand dunes.

And honestly, the noise usually doesn't bother me. When it's cold, nothing moves. But when there's a crowd of them, like today, and it's hot... I'll admit it is difficult to pretend that noise is just the wind. There must be thousands out there, writhing, jumping, trying to rush the compound.

My stage name was Ludvigo the Great. People call me Lou, but I am, was, and will always be Ludvigo the Great. I am with the Cirque. Of course, the world has come to an end, so regular performances have been postponed. But still, there is always the need for Ludvigo. The world provides these opportunities, and I have no choice but to seize them.

And thus, I hang three stories above the VIP pool at the Zanzibar Hotel and Casino.

This is nothing. I've been much higher before. Like the video where I free-climbed a 42-story tower without a harness. I was a pole vaulter in the old country and represented them in the Olympics, but that's not how the scout found me. It was when I danced at the top of the skyscraper like an angel on the head of a pin. These gifts I have require me to live life differently from most people. Maybe that's why I'm still alive, and they're undead. I live like I have nothing to lose. And they died sitting on their couches, watching the end of the world on a screen.

I dangle above the ground with tension wires clipped to my shoulders and back. I'm squirmy and slumped over, trying to appear hurt. Looking weak is a stretch for Ludvigo the Great, but I'm a consummate performer.

I wait for their final push. The crew has set up enough traps to take out ten thousand shamblers, but there needs to be real human bait, and that's my job.

We're quite a collection, those who lived—the acrobats, the bare-knuckle boxers, the bodyguards. We're led by an author named Maxwell. Can you believe he teaches unconventional war tactics at West Point? Or used to, at least. I wonder how the grunts at West Point are doing. Probably not bad in the winter. We can't be the last survivors in the world, even though it feels like it.

I look around the pool area. Once upon a time, this was the place to be. "A toptional oasis," reads the faded sandwich board sign, with privacy hedges protecting the view from the rest of the resort. Staff handed out special holographic wristbands and invited guests to get comfortable. The bare boobs often belonged to professional sex workers or those in the cuck and bull scene. No judgment, as I've been a part of both. Life is but a performance, and this was easy living. My gaze lingers on the tables inside the cabanas, where they used to deliver buckets of ice-cold coconut waters. Good clean fun. Well, not always clean. But I can't remember the last time I had any fun. Today's performance aside.

Static crackles in my earpiece. It's Maxwell's reassuring tenor.

"All right, Lou, look alive. You're on in roughly 60 seconds."

"Alive, I need to look? Why? Do I look dead?"

Maxwell chuckles. He appreciates gallows humor.

"Just look slightly less dead than your new friends over there."

The gate in front of me strains under a critical load of zombies pressing up the stairwell.

There's a zippered pouch in the middle of my chest, over my heart. Inside it, I keep my father's cigarette case. He was a welder behind the Iron Curtain. And he forged it out of some crazy alloy. Nickel Cobalt, he would say, ideal for extreme conditions. There are no conditions more extreme than this. Don't worry about the old man. He died well before all this. I take out a Marlboro Light and spark it. I always save one for right before a performance. It relaxes me. I lower my safety goggles. What's going to happen needs eye protection.

Just before the chaos hits, the hissing is almost overwhelming. I think about my cat, Fatty, who'd hiss and pat me when I tried to force him into the carrier. I let him free when the world ended. I know he's fine out there, cats are survivors. He probably lost a couple pounds, but we all did.

I flick the cig at the crowd, and the orange ashes bounce off a wayward ribcage. 100 points. The zombies don't notice.

A claxon horn blares and the metal gate buzzes open, letting loose a flood of zombies trampling over each other to get a piece of Ludvigo the Great. Easy, friends, easy, I have something extra special for my most dedicated fans. I extend two cans of bear mace toward the nearest biter and let them have both barrels.

That zombie and about a dozen nearby disintegrate into a pink powdery mist upon contact. It's the capsaicin in the spray. Maxwell figured it out, the genius that he is. We've been growing ghost peppers in every windowsill, seeds found in an abandoned Secret Santa gift in one of the penthouse suites. Thank God for whatever frat bro didn't eat the ghost pepper. Or thank Maxwell, more like it.

"Okay, Lou, you're looking good, and we're moving on to phase two."

"Copy that," I say, feeling the cans run light. The spice stings my nostrils. For a fancy military guy, Maxwell never says over. It doesn't matter anymore. I want to plead and beg, get me out of here, for the love of all that is holy, but that's beneath a performer of my stature. So I use nonsense phrases like "Copy that."

I breathe. I think of Fatty, loafed out low, tabby butt-wiggling, hunting birds. He's fine. I'm fine. Another sunny day in paradise. It's faith. So I close my eyes.

And just before their icy, jagged fingertips can snag a piece of Ludvigo, the wires retract, raising me out of harm's way. Like so many lemmings, the zombie mob pushes forward, crushing each other without regard. Empty eye sockets stare upward at me, Ludvigo, and my unparalleled body control. They don't have liquid to spare. No one does in this unrelenting desert. But if they did, these zombies would be drooling with undead hunger.

Of course, they don't see that they're charging headlong into a pool full of what can only be described as ghost pepper salsa. They never see the traps. The explosions start, like pops of confetti. From above, it's beautiful, a blizzard of pink snow. The dust from the first victims proves deadly to those behind. The zombies caught in the crush show the tiniest glimmer of concern, their posture fighting against the tide. But it's far too late for anything like that.

Can an animated skeleton show emotion? I argue yes. Like Fatty. They're nonverbal, but if you live with them for long enough, you can tell when they're pissed. As the wires reach the highest height, there's nothing horrible about these zombies at all. They're climbing on top of each other just for a piece of my shoe. Like a pop star. They will tear me apart. It might be the wildest crowd I ever performed for. And that's saying a lot for Ludvigo.

Illustration by Samuel Burbury Hanchett

Winter appears in the desert at night. The cold slows down the enemy, and that's when Maxwell orders out the scavenge teams. Ten days after the pool raid, I'm outside again.

It's early, and the glow of sunrise pushes against the mountains. Zanzibar is at the southern end of the Strip. It's a ten minute walk from massive plots of land like the airport and the LED-covered stadium. So, if you look in the right direction, you can see the big distance stretch over the horizon. It's a meditative feeling—like you're all alone.

But of course, Ludvigo is not alone; I am with the stilt walkers, a dozen Moko Jumbie from the Virgin Islands. We all know enough English, but they don't speak, either to each other or to me. And that's fine. Together we pick through pink piles of the double dead. We move slow and with great caution.

There are no "alive" zombies out here, but anything sharp remains deadly. A skull often has one final snap left in it, like a bear trap in the forest. So Maxwell sends out the stilt walkers, trained in their art well before the Cirque picked them up. I am an acrobat, a pole vaulter, and an overall lover of danger. When it comes to the stilts, Ludvigo learns faster than most.

I have a reacher-grabber in one hand and a black contractor bag in the other. These are more like skeletons than your traditional zombies. Just bones and sinew click-clacking a journey to Vegas. They seem harmless. Yet we all know a fall into the sharp pile would be a death sentence.

The world ended months ago, and we've never felt short of resources. You'd be surprised what the enemy carries into our traps. For all this talk about the apocalypse, surprisingly, the essentials haven't been a problem.

Parliaments, scotch, non-dairy coffee creamer. What's this, wrapped around half a jawbone. Night-vision goggles? It's incredible what zombies bring—the items they think they'll need in Vegas. Do they think? If so, what do they think about? The dog-eared copy of Dostoevsky's "The Brothers Karamazov" I carefully tweeze into my pouch prompts only more questions. The Grand Inquisitor was covered in blood.

What compelled them here? Is it muscle memory? Gambling addictions from beyond the grave? The execution of vacation plans crafted months before? I fill up the bin and make sure the magnet is set. I pull the steel rope twice. A few seconds later, the brutes on 61 start winching our newest treasures to the high ground.

In this life, if there's one thing Ludivgo knows, it's that "Why" is a greedy question to ask. None of this makes any sense. Survivors don't have the luxury of asking why the zombies come to Vegas in waves. Why they bring fun-sized Skittles, or why they come at all.

We'll never figure it out.

So, yeah. We figured it out.

I wake in my suite on 37 this morning and open the curtains. An unimaginable throng of zombies, maybe a million, clog the Strip, the stadium parking lot, legions of them. The mobs stretch in every direction.

The zombies are flocking in enormous numbers for something called the Super Bowl. Previously unknown to Ludvigo, this event is like the World Cup and the Olympics combined. And apparently, because the regular season was suspended due to the global apocalypse, delusional zombie fans of all the teams have arrived.

Another unsolved mystery is how, despite having hollow skulls empty of brain material, they all seem to have timed the journey

DESERT RAIN

on foot over months to arrive simultaneously. Maybe they didn't. Maybe ten million turned to dust along the way.

The world flashes. I think it's a nuke, but then my eyes clear. And I can't help but chuckle. Somehow, they got the LED stadium to light back up. It's cycling through test patterns. These zombies, they are like ants: stupid and harmless as individuals, but enough of them gather, and you're well and truly screwed.

It dawns on me: the fancy LED stadium connects to the Zanzibar. It's the only convenient way to get to the stadium. The whole compound was designed to funnel eighty thousand drunk whales through the casino floor, beyond the giant sportsbook video screen, down a marble hallway filled with luxury shops (AKA the mall-way), and then another ten minute walk, leading to the stadium itself. And then back again, four hours drunker. There is no other real way to get to the stadium. Unless you're emerging from the mountains like some sort of yeti and crossing ten lanes of walled interstate. Human or zombie, the Zanzibar is the only option.

I look down, and the casino design lives up to its potential. It's like New Year's Eve down there. The atrium entrances are packed with shamblers, crowded eight deep. They mostly wear jerseys, once vibrant, now sun-bleached rags, hats, and numbers hanging off bones. Their oversized chrome chains gleam in the sunlight. They shove against each other, spilling into the Zanzibar casino floor in unthinkable quantities.

My spine shivers in fear. That never happens to Ludvigo. This is bleak. I throw on the radio headphones, and the panicked chatter confirms everything I already know in my bones.

The casino is indeed overwhelmed, as are the stairwells. Despite throwing kegs of spice down the elevator shafts, they continue to climb. No one knows exactly how, but the leading theory is sheer brute force. Voices debate whether to load the sprinkler system with the last of the hot sauce. However, we all know that the cisterns on the roof are also our primary source of drinking water. Out here in the desert, it's trading a quick death for a slow one.

The line goes silent. Maxwell says nothing, probably digesting the bleak updates.

I sense the moment. The one we all knew would come. It is the last stand. The final countdown. And my fear shiver goes away. I know what comes next. You can't have a grand finale without Ludvigo the Great.

"Maxwell, send the winch down to my room," I say while putting on my dangler costume. "Room 3726."

"Do as he says," Maxwell says. I detect a tone of gratitude, a stoicism. This is a man settled to his fate. The Captain, ready to go down with his ship. But perhaps I'm only imagining all that color in Maxwell's words. It's up to the performer to create their own reality and invite the audience into it. Right now, I'm making a reality where I save all humanity. Or at least the remnant of it that's holed up in the Zanzibar.

An audience doesn't have to be millions of paying fans. One friend is more than enough.

Just as I finish zipping up my fly suit, the steel-roped magnet clanks against my glass. In what should be a shock to no one, Vegas lies about the floor numbers. It's only six stories between 63, the rooftop, where Maxwell surveys, and my humble nest on 37. The architects skipped about twenty floors to make the fancy floors seem fancier. Without other towers nearby, there was no point of reference, so no one really noticed the difference.

I take the business end of my carbon fiber vault pole, the lower half, and bash the window to the outside. I kick through the safety glass, and the gust almost takes me out into the desert sky. Not yet, goddess of the wind, not yet.

I take the winch and tie it around the handle of the fridge.

DESERT RAIN

"Only charge the magnet on my signal. Copy that?"

A crackle, and then Maxwell answers deliberately. "Yes, Ludvigo the Great, we copy."

I smirk. Max called me by my stage name. He used the radio jargon. He thinks we're all going to die.

But that's not good enough for Ludvigo. I can't have these bad vibes before a performance. The audience must be engaged for the magic to have its full effect.

In the before times, my hotel room would have been considered poor because it was so close to the elevator. Now, I thank this quirk of fortune because it gives me time before my greatest (and perhaps final) stunt to make one last speech.

I enter the hallway and take ten steps. I press my ear to the cold metal. Even with the elevator doors closed, I hear the undead heap below: hissing, clacking, churning upward.

Before I crowbar open the shaft, I open my Nickel-Cobalt case and spark my last Marlboro Light. It's time to make peace with this life.

"Hey. HEY! To everyone on the radio: now is the time to listen to Ludvigo the Great. I have good news. Raise your eyes. Wipe your tears. Spare your blood. Because even though we all die in this world, today is not that day! Today, we live!

"Oh sure, maybe you don't believe me. That's fine, my friends, you will. And when all this is over, you will pour Ludvigo a drink, shake his hand, and thank him for this miracle he's about to create from nothing but wind and sky... and shaman magic from the old country. Please, I need silence, this will be my greatest trick and requires total concentration."

I don't really need silence, it's a great line though. I jack open the doors with a crowbar and shove an old room service cart in the maw to keep it from closing. One last deep drag then toss my lit cigarette butt. The light from the falling fire tells me the undead horde pack is only about three floors down, close enough to see their lanyards. I can see the pink shimmers. Around their necks are platinum club players' cards.

These zombies gambled enough to earn comped rooms during Super Bowl weekend. That's an obscene amount of players' points to accumulate in any lifetime. It's not like these fictional units of measurement accrue interest.

I let out an involuntary "huh" sound, as for once, the motivation of these creatures makes a strange sense. These unholy aberrations aren't after our brains. Well, yes, they are obviously yearning for our juicy, delicious brains. But besides that, these particular suspects were made a promise in their past lives by the morally nebulous corporation formerly known as Zanzibar Gaming LLC.

Those in the elevator shaft have returned from beyond the desert and perhaps the very border between life and death to get what they are owed. Every tourist in Vegas is obsessed with a trip to the top of the building, the penthouse suite. Who's got the sweetest suite? Even if it's twenty stories shorter than everyone believes.

I get that. Like James Brown, they want the big payback. They need revenge. That and the meaty smell of Maxwell's human encampment on 63 motivates them to do the impossible. These zombies escape gravity by creating a new tower for Babel. By zombies, for zombies, made of zombies.

Who knows what they are truly capable of? Give them a couple more years; maybe I can finally get that plane ride back to the old country. Or a raft at least.

For now, they only want to rise and are consumed by it. They don't know it yet, but I have something they'll want even more. I take my boot knife and cut my arm, letting it drip down my hands, my fingertips, and into the void.

The hissing intensifies. Zombie frames crackle and lurch, stretching tall toward the service cart. Yes, my sweeties, let's take this party back to my room.

It's fun, showering my blood down on a writhing tower of doom. But it's only when I step back from the elevator that I notice the troubling amount of blood spurting out of my left arm.

I laugh grimly. Here, I was frightened I wouldn't have enough bait to lure away an entire casino's worth of zombies. I trail blood back to my room and realize that I don't have that concern anymore.

Red blood sprays around the suite. I nicked a vein. I wrap gray duct tape around my arm. It doesn't really stick. But I keep wrapping. It will be fine. This is fine. Certainly, it's not going to stop my most fantastic performance ever.

I'm not lightheaded, not yet. But I'm not worried, either. When it comes to that, Maxwell surely will winch me back up to the rooftop, where my depleted body can be restored with cool, nourishing coconut water. Like soldiers in the Pacific theater. Or the cabanas at the VIP pool.

And if he can't bring me back, I'm ready for that too. A samurai must think of death every day and always be prepared for it.

I hold the winch in one hand and the zipper chest pocket with my father's Nickel-Cobalt cigarette case in the other.

"Okay, Maxwell," I say. "Light me up."

I gasp as the winch grips the extremely magnetic material in the cigarette case. It's a deep, bone-rattling vibration through my ribcage, grabbing my very soul. Like when I used to stand atop the subwoofers and dance at the casino nightclub.

There's an awkward bang at the door, and without looking behind me, I know my first guests have arrived. I grab my vault pole, both halves this time, then run and leap through the open window, through the air outside the room.

I assume from the hissing that a crowd of shamblers has followed, drawn by my blood. I make the mistake of looking down and catch the sight of my blood dripping off my boot, a concerning amount, falling forty stories, spreading like mist across the desert below.

"It's fine," I say aloud, "the human body is mostly water." I attach the two halves of the pole, making a grand total of five meters. This carbon fiber baby launched me to many a personal best. Some athletes name their poles, usually a pithy blues guitar name like Suzy Q or Mabel. I never disrespected my instrument in this way. It is an it, not a he, she or they. And that's fine. It is a champion. I know this pole with an intimacy that is unrivaled. I have taken it apart and put it back together countless times, before and after practices and meets, dozens assemblies a day for years on end. Therefore, I can do it with my eyes closed. Or with them open, while hanging from a winch, slowly bleeding out.

"Hello, old friend," I say as I grab the pole and use it to balance myself against the steel beams of the hotel tower.

Then I swing back and forth, laughing, jumping and poking the nearest zombie. I start to trip them, hook their feet, and check them into the glass as they fall. I hear cheers over the radio. No, that's not right. The radio isn't on.

I look up, and the cheers come from the roof. I smile and wiggle the pole. Then I hear crunching noises like when my grandmother broke crackers into my soup broth as a kid. I look down. Turns out my adoring crowd on the roof is nothing compared to the ultimate waterfall of carnage I'm creating over the pool, parking garage, and ride-share pickup area of the once mighty Zanzibar Hotel and Casino.

Hundreds of zombie corpses turn into thousands, turn into tens of thousands. Snap, Crackle, and Pop. Shards fly. They keep coming. Up and out. It's a mountain of pink dust, swirling up from the ground. The dust mixes with my blood, creating a tasty mist. Like an expensive restaurant dish made from foam. They're diving

 DESERT RAIN

to their second deaths for cotton candy. Their corpse pile below writhes in pleasure.

After a while, traffic starts to thin. And I can't bounce like before, I mostly lean against the pole and winch, standing on air.

Drip, drop. I'm officially sick. Woozy.

I'm dying, for sure. No, I'm not bleeding out. It took Jesus three days to empty out, hanging on the cross. Yeah, but didn't they give him water on a sponge or something? I would kill for a sponge.

I close my eyes. Just a short rest. The winch starts to retract, but I don't feel it. I don't feel anything but the bliss of the fallen hero. I get why people do it. It's a warm feeling like you matter. Like the sun on your face in a cabana. I don't even need the coconut water anymore.

It's fine. It's nice. You can do a lot worse.

It doesn't matter if you fall asleep and never wake up if the last thought you have is that you saved everyone.

Illustration by Samuel Burbury Hanchett

A ZOMBIE DISPATCH

by Derek Davis

THE ZOMBIES I'VE KNOWN ARE, FOR THE MOST PART, UNCOMMUNICATIVE.

Being technically dead, though undead by convention, they have lost much of their cognitive function, and their concerns are chiefly killing and eating, offset somewhat by their surprising fondness for dogs as pets, whom they feed with cast-off parts of themselves. This has led to an almost sappy bond between owner and keeper, with no clear demarcation as to which is which.

But within any group there are always exceptions, some to the downside, some to the up. What I'm presenting below are the words penned by my zombie... "buddy" is a bit of an overstatement, but "acquaintance" is shy of the mark. I'll just say friend and leave the interpretation to you.

My friend's name is Surfer, or perhaps Surefire. For reasons that he claims are "purely zombic," he refuses to spell out his name in writing, and his verbal rendition is rather uncertain from the decay of his lips and throat. He can, however, type competently, if slowly on my MacBook—wearing gloves to protect the keys. In this case, he has produced an engaging, if perhaps not socially acceptable, insider report on zombie behavior. I make no comment as to its accuracy. This is his story, not mine.

Hi! My uphill neighbor Derek has asked me to write a note to let people know more about how zombies go about daily existence and help clear up some of the stereot—I can never remember the whole word—about our "lifestyle." I should say right here at the beginning, that I would never eat Derek's brain because he always keeps his head up his ass. That's a joke.

Yes, we do eat brains, both because we believe they help us replace thought power lost through dying and reanimating—a tough process, let me tell you—and because they're soft and easy to chew, especially once our teeth begin to fall out. However, we do not eat whole heads! Skulls have some of the thickest bones in the body, and we have a devil of a time breaking them loose without a pry-bar and chisel. Some of my fellow zombies bash in the skull with a hammer, but I find that the dust and chips that fall in cheapen the flavor.

Our group feasts have gotten an unfortunately bad name. I want to make it clear that we do not constantly rampage, biting and drooling and generally making a mess in the streets. But like anybody, live or undead, there are times when we become enraged at how some so-called "normal" livies behave toward us. Livies can be very unfriendly, throwing things at us or running away screaming instead of stopping to talk and get to know us. When this sort of thing gets out of hand... well, not surprisingly, so do we.

Oh, I should stop to say more about our feasts, so this account does not come across as just another bad-tempered rant. We do eat vegetables. I personally prefer broccoli, which goes surprisingly well with a spicy cranium madras. Our zombie jamborees often feature Zombie Jambalaya. Fresh blood with cream soda and a dash of celery makes a delicious dinner beverage, best if cooled to just this

    A ZOMBIE DISPATCH

side of congealing. A great deal of the blood we drink, by the way, is purchased from embalmers. (Outright slaughter, as I've been trying to impress, is frowned upon when not provoked.) Dessert usually features entrails, including my favorite, I Never Saw Such Sausage.

What do we do for fun? Well, as you might suspect, copulation is simply impossible when your sexual organs tend to disintegrate during any extended activity. But we do tell "raunchy" stories to provide mental release. Playing cards or board games?—same thing, alas. But thank Decay for the internet. If we lay a plastic sheet over the keyboard to prevent gumming, there's nothing better than an evening of zombie games like Great Gore Almighty, Graveyard Crawl or Over the Liver and Through the Spleen.

I guess I should also explain that zombies don't really prefer night activity, it's just that we never sleep. Whatever part of the brain controls sleep seems to be the first to go, so it's 24 hours a day awake, so we need a lot of food to sustain us, even as our matab— metab—lost the word again—slows down (and eventually stops, which leads to dead-undeadness).

I know, I've made zombie "life" (ha ha) sound boring, but at least there are a lot of us, so each has a good chance of finding others with a similar personality type to hang around with. On the down side, since every time we bite a livey they turn into a zombie, it can get crowded in the basements where we spend most of our daytime hours. When that starts to happen, we enforce a rule: "Eat only the dead," though it's admittedly hard to enforce in practice.

Well, I think that's enough about who we are and how we spend our time, but I do want to add that I'm darned lucky to have a live friend like Derek. He's unusual in having no antipathy to zombies as long as we respect certain limits, That might even be a good idea for world peace. Of course, we zombies tend to be in worldwide pieces.

Illustration by Samuel Burbury Hanchett

THE CHILDREN

by Derek Davis

THE CHILDREN WERE NOT MUTE but devoid of intelligence. They stood in a single row, side by side, facing the street with its abandoned trolley tracks. Years before, machines had rattled by, but now the neighborhood was not deemed worthy of such amenities.

The children had once been like others, with a range of mental abilities and degrees of a zest for life. But they had gone wrong—their leaders from perversity of character, the followers from weakness of will. They had been punished. They had been rendered mentally sterile, much as, years before, rapists had been rendered physically sterile through castration. Some did not know their names. Those that did could not say what it meant to have a name. I was their keeper.

I could not remember how this had come to be, no more than they could remember their origins and deeds. We had arisen in the same time, I surmised, and were linked in some inevitable way. At nights it made me weep, but during the day I stood by them and directed their movements as a puppetmaster might direct his marionettes.

At the time of which I speak, we were waiting for transportation. Not from the defunct trolleys, of course, but from some unidentified conveyance that would soon appear to take us to the bathing ponds.

There the children would be cleansed, physically, but their minds would remain unchanged. Forever, they would be as they were now, growing older but neither wiser nor more accomplished.

None of the children moved as we waited. Most looked straight ahead, as though plugged firmly into the ground, like trees. But Louis occasionally shifted his eyes, right and left, up and down. Louis knew his name and, I suspected, other details as well. He had been the ringleader, or so I had been told at a time which now eludes me. Louis had been, perhaps, a psychopath in the making. He had delighted in leading the others astray, in shifting reality to bring it into conflict with the lives of those around him. I do not know why I use that expression, it comes from somewhere in the past. I knew Louis before his change. Of that much I feel certain.

We had been waiting for at least an hour. It made no difference to the children. If the wait was too long for their physical bodies, they would simply drop and fall asleep. Yet, as the wait increased, a subtle fear—no, apprehension rather—stole over me. I had been misinformed about some detail, this skittishness seemed to say, that would be our undoing.

I studied the street in order to divert my mind. Between the tracks the asphalt had been gashed and chipped away, as though gnawed by some gigantic rodent. The corners of glazed, almost iridescent brick peeked through. What sort of neighborhood had this been in its heyday? For an instant I could see the sway of the trolley cars, hear the laughter of their riders on their way to some welcome event, but as quickly as it had come, the vision passed.

After I tired of studying the decay around me, I attempted to push my mind back in time, but beyond what I might deem three years, it reached a wall of confusion. There was no abrupt disappearance of memory, but a turbulence, like fog rolling in across a lake. It angered me for some reason, this dimness, though I had encountered it a hundred times before without particular rancor. What was my offense, that I had been set upon so, kept from normal activity and self-history

THE CHILDREN

and put in charge of a mindless troop of former rogues? And what was their offense to be condemned for all of life while yet so young? This could not be justice. Justice must include understanding and a sense of consequence.

A slight rumble approached, and along the track appeared a handcar pumped by two figures in clown suits, polka-dotted and alive with whimsy. They pushed the bars of the handcart with exaggerated rhythm, as though playing a massive organ. Of a sudden, both stopped their motion and the car rolled to a halt before us.

One of the clowns leapt down and bowed. The other threw his hands high and uttered a razzberry, then blew his nose into the street, issuing a copious stream of snot.

The clown in the street pointed to the sky, then to the earth. He pirouetted in his oversized shoes and hiccuped loudly, ripped the clown mask from his face, dropped to all fours and snarled. The mask beneath—or was it his face?—was elongated and acned, a horrible visage to look upon but somehow comforting. He was our true father. That idea flashed before me, unbidden. My body longed to bow, but I refused its pull. He replaced his clown mask and snickered.

Both clowns cavorted before us, but the children did not react. Nor did I. They could not, I would not. I was enraged that such travesties would make sport of a collective infirmity—which was none of our doing. I wished that I could bring down on them a fire of wrath. Yet their laughter was soothing and I fell into a melancholy of the sort that can relax the mind. I thought of my mother and wondered how it could be that I remembered her when I could remember nothing else of my past. My mother rose gigantic in my mind, a towering figure with a tiny waist and a simpering walk. She bent down to hand me a cookie. A fly settled on it before I could bring it to my mouth.

One of the clowns pointed down the track, in the direction from which they had come, and screamed, a high animal squeal. Both clowns jumped on the handcar and pumped away into the distance.

I could see nothing where they had pointed. It was the street, as the street had been, devoid of traffic and peopled by no one. One of the children began to cry. I had never heard this before. I welled with panic. What else might they be capable of, what bursts of emotion and incipient frenzy that I could not hope to control?

The crying stopped and we waited. In time, from the direction the clowns had come, arrived two sedans and a limousine. A courtly figure with silver-white hair and a wry smile exited from the rear of the limousine. He bowed to the right, then to the left. He waved his hand toward the sedans. All four doors of both sedans opened to exhibit men in pinstriped suits and porkpie hats. Each held a weapon. Some wielded semi-automatic pistols, others sleek handguns. They aimed their weapons at the children and began firing. Singly and in groups, the children fell. They did not cry out but collapsed like fresh plaster falling off a wall. Their blood seemed both senseless and charismatic. They fell and did not move, but the masters of the weapons stepped forward and emptied round after round into their immobile bodies. The silver-haired man looked at me without expression and re-entered the limousine. The cars drove off without haste.

Now that my charges had been exterminated, would I be released? It was an ignoble question to harbor at such a time. Among the corpses, one child showed residual life. Louis fixed his eyes on me and the corners of his mouth attempted a smile. I could not return his acknowledgement, and that, more than the carnage, tore my heart.

THE CHILDREN

TOP 10 ZOMBIE FILM DIRECTORS OF ALL TIME

RANK	DIRECTOR	CONTIBUTIONS TO THE GENRE
1	George Romero (1940-2017)	Night of the Living Dead (1968) Dawn of the Dead (1978) Day of the Dead (1985) Land of the Dead (2005)
2	Sam Raimi (1959-)	Evil Dead (1981) Evil Dead II (1987) Army of Darkness (1992)
3	Edgar Wright (1974 -)	Shaun of the Dead (2004)
4	Yeon Sang-ho (1978-)	Train to Busan (2016) Peninsula (2020)
5	Danny Boyle (1967-)	28 Days Later (2002)
6	Zach Snyder (1966-)	Dawn of the Dead (2004) Army of the Dead (2021)
7	Peter Jackson (1961-)	Braindead (1992) AKA Dead Alive
8	Ruben Fleischer (1974-)	Zombieland (2009) Zombieland: Double Tap (2019)
9	Jaume Balagueró (1968-) & Paco Plaza (1973-)	REC (2007, 2009, 2012, 2014)
10	Stuart Gordon (1947-2020)	Re-Animator (1985)

HONORABLE MENTION

Lucio Fulci (1927-1996)	Zombie (1979) City of the Living Dead (1980)
Wes Craven (1939-2015)	The Serpent and the Rainbow (1988)
Juan Carlos Fresnadillo (1967-)	28 Weeks Later (2007)
Robert Rodriguez (1968-)	Planet Terror (2007)
Francis Lawrence (1971-)	I Am Legend (2007)
Marc Forster (1969-)	World War Z (2013)
André Øvredal (1973-)	The Autopsy of Jane Doe (2016)
Colm McCarthy (1973-)	The Girl With All The Gifts (2016)
Shin'ichirô Ueda (1984-)	One Cut of the Dead (2017)

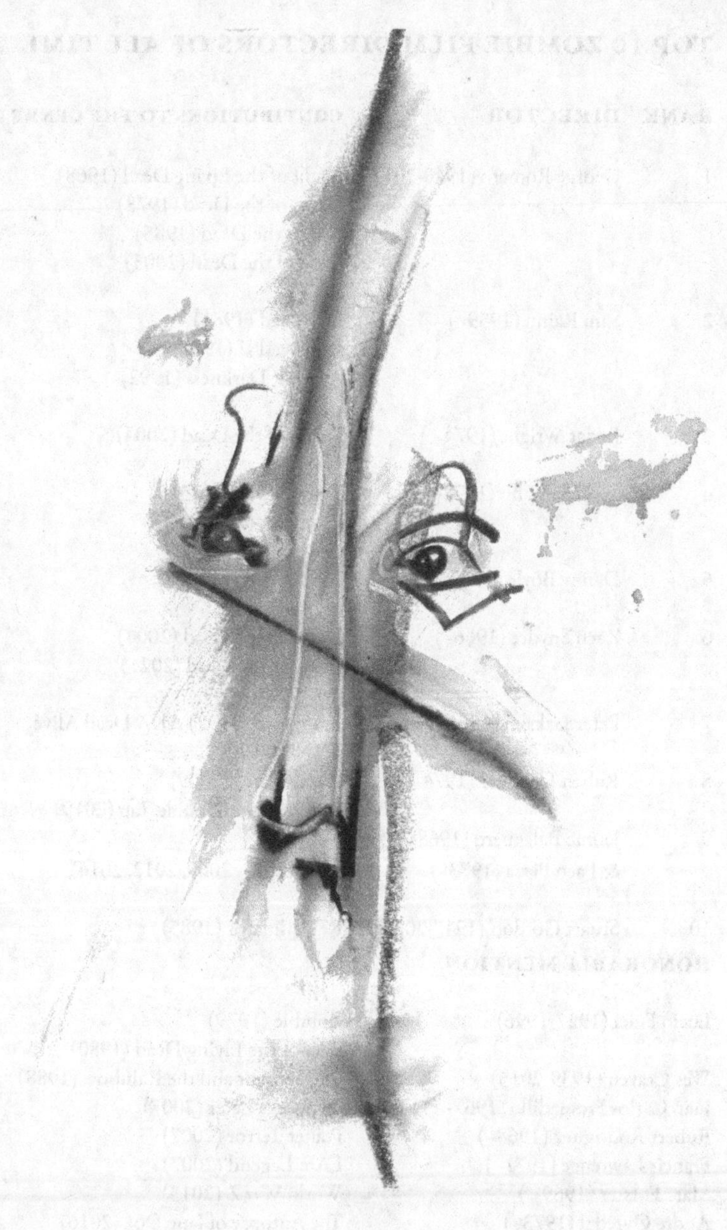

Illustration by Samuel Burbury Hanchett

PLANNED OBSOLESCENCE

by Ev I.L. Frazier

WIND SINGS THROUGH the openings of a worn down house. Fluid drips through unseen cracks. The ragdoll man sleeps restlessly. His eyes flutter as he rises to the surface, beckoned by the dripping. Has the roof rotted through again? As his eyes open he sees that his roof is whole. Crimson drips from his bloodstained arm, pooling beneath his bed. He sits up, taking a closer look. A new crack runs down his forearm. His skin is chipped and brittle like porcelain.

The man groans. He rises to his feet and lumbers to the bathroom, blood trailing behind him. On the sink sits a tub of plaster and a rusted scraper. With a practiced monotony he pops open the lid and scrapes out the last glob of off-white paste, using the tool and his fingers to clumsily fill the crack. Similar ragged streaks of moulding run along the curves of his body. How many were there? Ten? Twenty? Thirty? He had lost count. It happened practically every day now.

With the crack sealed, he continues his morning routine. He does not recognize the face staring from the mirror. Or rather, the facsimile of a face. Staples hold the flayed meat of his face together. Who knew that skin could just slide off the bone like that without being slow cooked first? In a panic, he had chosen to piece his facade back together with some readily available hot glue and a staple gun. Evidently poor tools for the task of reconstructing a countenance out of gristly Play-Doh.

Gray tiger stripes paint the body, criss crossing over medical stitching along his shoulder and waist—phantoms of the brief epoch where he could afford to visit a doctor for stopgap care. They poked and prodded and swabbed. Fascinated by the man's condition. But they offered no treatment. No Solutions. Only examination.

An unexpected windfall of an inheritance had once allowed him to seek out an out-of-network specialist. Someone who could hopefully identify what was causing him to unravel. But hopes were soon dashed amongst the stones. The specialist could not see what was wrong with the man. Perhaps he ought to just get more exercise and start eating better. The fact that two of the man's teeth had fallen out over the course of the appointment went unacknowledged. The man pleaded and begged with the specialist. An MRI. An X-ray. Something. Anything. Just please find out why he's gone rotten. A display of vulnerability so perverse that it would earn him being led off the premises by security.

He had never been a rich man, but his financial situation had only gotten worse as medical bills piled up and his hours at work whittled away. He had been pushed to the graveyard shift. A walking dead man. "It's for the best," his manager had said through a plastic smile.

With his income in tatters, he would be forced to find a new method to patch himself together with each new injury. A needle and thread to restrain his form to the shape of a man. But he was no seamstress. Fingers became askew. Skin was pinched and torn. The results became more and more patchwork with each suture. Eventually his hands were too misshapen to even thread the needle.

     PLANNED OBSOLESCENCE

Messy stitches became even messier moulding. The tub of plaster he emptied this morning joins a growing pile in the corner.

He opens the medicine cabinet and chokes down a series of painkillers. How he has not died of an infection he does not know, but nothing stops the pain. His skin and muscle and bone ache from the constant wear. His skull a constant thunderstorm of headaches.

He writhes and wiggles into his work clothes. A baggy hoodie and medical mask hide his horrid facade from his neighbors, his fellow passengers, his few coworkers. He had become nothing more than a tenuosuly useful shadow; a temporary tool to discard once worn to the bone. Losing utility by the day as his muscles gradually soften into putty. Was this really still the life of a person? Or had he transitioned into some unknowable purgatory? It did not change things either way. He would still need money. He would still need to keep himself together. He would still need to stock shelves. Until he couldn't, anyhow. His time at work is ending. This night shift is only a stopgap solution until he withers away completely. He knows this, but there is nothing he can do.

The night of work was over before he even knew it started. The warm glow of a new dawn paints the world in a heavenly image while he waits at the bus stop. This was the one pleasure he still indulged in— the sunrise after work. It was one of the only times he would see the sun at all before he slinked off to his nest for a difficult day of fitful sleep. However, before he slept, he needed to restock his depleted supplies.

As he arrives at the barely open hardware store, he shambles as quickly as he can to where the plaster usually is. He is greeted by an empty shelf. He checks a nearby kiosk. Out of Stock.

Panic creeps in. The man stumbles through aisles. Looking desperately for something that might keep him together. Hope presents itself in a roll of duct tape. How long would that last? A week? Less? He is not given the time to ponder as an employee approaches him gingerly. He had failed to notice the splatters of blood and molting flesh left in his wake.

"Sir, I'm going to have to ask you to leave," she says with that same plastic smile, "You're scaring the other customer."

The store is not busy yet, but the man understands. He finds himself scary too. He nods and shuffles out the door. Waiting for the bus, he takes out his wallet to retrieve his fare. However, a swift gust blows it and his hand away. It rolls along the ground, still gripping the worn leather, before falling into a storm drain with a wet plop. The man laughs, despite himself, and begins to walk towards the direction of home, leaving a red trail behind him.

     PLANNED OBSOLESCENCE

SENSI STAR

by Bertram Montiekowicz

[MALE VOICE, HOST]: "You want to test your sound?"

[FEMALE VOICE, GUEST]: "No, that's fine."

[HOST]: "All right, let's get started."

[intro music plays]

[HOST]: "Three, two, one... Welcome to tonight's edition of, 'You Bet Your Ass!'"

[intro music fades]

[HOST]: "I'm your host, Dinghy Doolittle, and today we have our most special guest ever. No one will ever see the kind of streaming numbers artists used to get before the Pop Drop, but it's comparable, percentage wise, to some of the greatest of all time! Why? Well, today the world gets to hear from one of its heroes for the first time.

"Born Carrie Ann Morgrona, you know her as Sensi Star. You probably heard her latest hit, 'You're So Careless,' almost a million have, but we're not here to talk about the hit-making machine. Today's topic is a little more serious than a man who is careless with his mate's feelings; I'm sure Ms. Star would agree.

"Sensi or Carrie, Ms. Morgrona is even more serious, I know our time is short, so let's get right to it. The human race credits you with winning the Zombie War, but you've refused to talk about it until now. Why, and why for the love of God would you agree to do this interview with me of all people?"

[GUEST]: "I don't like to talk about zombies, as everyone knows, I don't even like the term zombie, even though I find myself using it all the time when the subject comes up. Maybe that's why I don't like to talk about it."

[HOST]: "You sound a little angry."

[GUEST]: "That's why I'm here. I wanted to take a couple minutes and set the record straight. There's different stories making the rounds, everybody thinks they know. You either tell your own story or someone will do it for you."

[HOST]: "True, but why not just take a victory lap and call it done? Certainly there are plenty of clichés you could have reused, why not just 'Thank God for the opportunity' and move on?"

[pause]

[GUEST]: "Hopefully listeners have their answer as to why I chose your show for this interview."

[HOST, laughing]: "Let's not get too congratulatory just yet."

[HOST continues]: "Think about it. Everyone wants to be part of the victory lap, some more than the victory itself, which is filled with tension, while the victory lap is pure joy. This public stance

Illustration by Samuel Burbury Hanchett

you've taken, or lack of public stance, there must be some part of you that feels like you've betrayed your fans."

[GUEST]: "Fans make a choice like everybody else. My fans value authenticity, or at least I like to think they do. For me to be untrue to me would be the greatest betrayal my fans could suffer, and if that statement is false, how could they be my fans?"

[pause]

[HOST]: "We agreed I would ask the questions."

[GUEST]: "Sorry, I was being rhetorical."

[HOST]: "You threw me off. My goodness, we're running out of time already and I still haven't got to the point. You have to tell us, how did you do it? Everyone wants a share of success, even more than they want to avoid being part of a failure. Think of it as a tutorial for your fans. Certainly the zombie invasion will not be the last crisis humanity faces."

[pause]

[GUEST]: "To claim victory would be to forget those who gave their lives, who left clues. I had the means. Who else had access to a sound system capable of testing their theory on such a grand scale, who had contacts in the government, could work with the Army to feed the Slop? Who else could stage a live event to a global audience in the middle of a Zombie War? You think I want to be remembered for this? The credit should always go to the people who gave their life, and they are precisely the ones who never get to hear the word thanks. So why should I? To thank anyone else becomes an injustice. Think of Telford Taylor."

[HOST]: "The Fiddler."

[GUEST]: "For Taylor to play so beautifully with the zombies at his gate, not for the cameras, he didn't even know the drone was there. That was artistry. So anything I did is nothing compared to the sacrifice Taylor and others like him made. I never really risked my skin. Taylor is gone, but in giving his life he left behind a clue. He showed the world that the so-called zombie, that it hadn't lost its humanity, not completely. Taylor proved in this way we were alike, that the beauty of music operates on a different level. Music reaches our full brain in a way nothing else does. Sadly, for Telford, he hoped music would soothe the savage beast, but there was something else going on. Music proved the zombies had a humanity to restore. They call it a crime against humanity, but the crimes start when you deny someone their humanity. That's always the first step."

[HOST] "Sounds like 'We Are One.'"

[GUEST] "Trust me, the topic was very much on my mind when I wrote the song.

[GUEST, singing lyrics] 'You can't own me, you can't sell me; you can't clone me, you don't feel me.'"

[HOST, singing chorus] "'What will God say, when He sees what you've done to his image.'"

[HOST, continues] "One of my favorites. I'm sure the fans will be happy to hear you haven't completely given up singing live."

[GUEST] "I'd love to just be a pop star again, but that's not how it played for me. I'll always be the zombie killer. My celebrity resulted in me getting way more credit than I deserved. I learned from radio sleuths... Miron the Moron. I believe he was the first to speculate the zombies gravitated to big cities, not because they were drawn to Democratic mayors like the idiots on Fox News were claiming, but because they wanted to get away from the peaceful sounds of nature. Crickets are soothing to our animal brain, and as we all know now, this was the zombies' psychosis, they were tired of being soothed.

The most beautiful music in the world could not have soothed these savage beasts. But, the music had a certain control over them, they could be made to dance, and in that dance they found a release from the hunger that drove them to kill. They went into the dance freely, and often could be danced into a state of exhaustion; that wasn't me who learned that. The song we chose had to be long enough to produce the effect. It wasn't me who found they were so starving when they woke they would actually try to eat the Slop. Think of how many Caregivers gave their lives to learn that simple fact. If you had enough Slop they would just eat and eat and eat until they threw up, and then they passed out again, felt a little bit better when they woke, entered a more placid state. This was all known to me. If you had enough Slop, you could keep feeding them and feeding them and eventually their bodies would reboot the ability to gain weight. Only then would they stop trying to eat you. Behind every zombie was that hunger. Deaden the hunger, kill the zombie, not the person, but what they had become. You want to make a hero out of me, it's not going to stick. The hero was Steph, bringing me hot tea at one in the morning, the people who showed up to work when all seemed lost. They're the heroes. I had a team behind me; that's who wins, it's never one person... see, you got your cliché after all."

[HOST]: "Thank you, my job is done! Seriously, though, at least you have to admit, it was you who chose to use the song, 'Killing in the Name of' by Rage Against the Machine?"

[GUEST]: "Right, well, we were on the Battle of LA pretty quick, it was just a question of which song. The tempo changes are properly sequenced. Rage, I mean, from the first meeting we were pretty much convinced it would have to be a Rage song, but the key was you had to be able to listen to it over and over and over without it losing any of its luster. After we lost the Internet, it had to be a song most people could find on disc and cassette. It had to be something from the '90s. The Army was standing by with the Slop, so the lyrics had to address that power. They call it the Zombie War but it was

    SENSI STAR

a revolt. The men in uniform had to accept there's nothing more American than filling the streets and demanding bread. Remember, if you didn't have any Slop to feed the zombies after the dance, they would just keep coming back. The music had to keep playing while they were sleeping. When the zombies first woke, that was the only time you could scare them with sound, the Army figured that out when the war first started. So people who didn't have tons of Slop would just chase the zombies away. That meant boomboxes. I hear all the time, even you, saying the old government was totally useless, but they brought in trainloads of batteries when we needed them the most, Cs, Ds, nine volts. We'd still be fighting if it wasn't for that. They say it's always the supplies that win the war. The execution of some of these musical assault teams, switching from one boombox to another to make sure the song never ended, reloading the batteries, keeping the tapes dry, as we used to say. Deep in the forest the assault teams could retreat, let the sweet sound of nature do the rest. Let the birds and crickets take up the fight, the babbling brook, peace and harmony, no inequality. You looking for heroes? How about the chick with the walkman, who had the gut to slip the headphones on a zombie when he was sleeping, danced with him all the way, then went back for another. Only in nature could the so-called zombie sleep, and dream. I agree with those who say that was the big thing, lack of REM, the lack of good sleep, science doesn't have to understand everything; we die without our dreams. It's my theory, these days everybody has one. There was no way to ask the zombies about their dreams. I mean, I get it, there would have never been even one zombie if so many people hadn't run out of food, money, medicine, shelter. Now the wilderness is theirs, people have started calling them Elves. 'The Elves'll get you in the woods.' I guess it never ends, there's always someone being demonized."

[HOST]: "What do you think it was about that particular song?"

[GUEST]: "Mentally, I mean, obviously I'm no brain surgeon, but this idea that once we already like a song, our brain treats it differently, it's neither short or long term memory, it's simply right there, accessible, because our mind likes it, wants to keep it close. This is why everyone can recite the lyrics of their favorite song verbatim at any time even if they can't remember anything else."

[HOST]: "Good stuff. And, don't go anywhere, we'll be right back after a quick word from our sponsors."

[jaunty music, fade to commercial break]

A horde of zombies huddle and surge.

"Some of us remember... "

The voice-over has a bit of a raspy edge, like he has a few holes in his throat, but it is that radio announcer voice, full of basso and profundo...

A zombie finds a quarter, stands in front of a laundry machine, its clothes are in the machine, they tumble without water.

"You have to take what you can find."

Zombies toiling through the mall full of mold and dust.

"But you have to look for the best."

A pile of clean 501 jeans.

"If you don't know what to look for, you'll be stuck with the rest."

The horde moves through shambling and groaning...

In a store, a gang of zombies pause beside the denim, a zombie girl is trying on a pair of Levi's. A zombie guy is buttoning a jacket up in a lazy half forgotten vestigial fashion.

"What is going to outlast the others."

The zombie troupe looks bad ass now, they have levis and helmets and sunglasses on.

　　　　　　　　SENSI STAR

"It takes us a while in this life to figure it out... "

The zombie girl looks at herself in the mirror which is cracked and dusty, but what she sees is herself as she remembers herself.

The zombie group of badasses roll out into the sun-baked landscape with their new 501's, and pass the narrator as he says,

"But we stick to what lasts, and what lasts, stays with us."

He is standing with his own zombie gang, their 501s, though stained and torn, have clearly been worn forever.

"That's Levi's Loyalty."

[more jaunty music, talk show returns]

[HOST]: "Look, I have to ask you this, what about this accusation people are making, that you forgive the zombies for everything they did, even what happened to your sister?"

[pause]

[GUEST]: "Are we still getting our feelings hurt? What is left of a person when they are so starved they start eating brains? Then act surprised they like it warm? The zombies' brains were deficient, lacking in protein, and this grayness is why they wouldn't bother trying to eat each other, it's like living on lettuce. You know all this. You want to know why I forgive? If you think of zombies like people, maybe you see where they're coming from. The zombies were far past the point of lecturing, beyond facts and rationales, propaganda. They had no faith in the ballot box, the Bible. What is truth to a generation raised by lies? Zombies don't care about peace and love and understanding, or war and hate and treason. The words of the American president had been made cheap. The zombies were coming at everything from a different viewpoint. I don't think it's fair to judge people, any people. We're all flawed, stumbling into our next mistake, trying to act like we didn't do anything wrong... all of which to say, forgiveness is often all we have to offer, especially during wartime. You asked me to come on your show, to honor me, my accomplishments, but if I did not forgive the zombies for killing my sister, and many others who were close to me, dear to me, people whose loss is like an abyss that I'm skirting even now, like I'm on the edge of it, and ready to fall down there, where they went, and I'm not afraid of the journey, it's the destination, that's the problem. Think about that, what comes next is a place where we never see each other again anyway, the emptiness, each of us, you, me, we all have our own little patch of blackness waiting for us, our whole lives, just waiting to go in that box. You understand what I'm trying to say? Whether I had a hit song or won the Zombie War or whatever anyone does, it doesn't matter, nothing matters. So yeah, forgive all, because life's too short."

[pause]

[HOST]: "Would it be fair to paraphrase what you're saying as, without forgiveness, we would still be fighting, that wars can only be won when combatants care about their enemy?"

[GUEST]: "I guess. To reach the zombies meant first accepting they had just cause, that what we become is never completely our fault. The afterlife I described, a nothingless, looked good. They tuned out the media, the experts, the government. The Army used sound as a weapon, leaving many deafened and harder to reach. The song's bassline was key, because even the deaf needed to feel the music."

[ping]

                    SENSI STAR

[HOST]: "And just like that we're out of time. Thank you so much for doing this interview, Sensi, I really mean that, and it's not just the money you made me. I doubt you were able to set the record straight, or if that's possible in the times we live in. No one believes assertion or contrition. Now, before we go, we agreed to one question at random, so here goes, and I'll leave the last word to you. The question is from Snarky1point5, 'Thank you Sensi Star for helping end the Zombie War. My question is, who do you think was the first zombie ever?'"

[GUEST]: "I guess you weren't listening Snarky. I don't want your thanks, and I don't appreciate being baited. I wasn't trying to save humanity, only myself. That's what I did, I saved myself. If we all did the same, well, humanity would be saved, wouldn't it? I'm sure you think because I supported prison emancipation that I bear some of the blame for the Zombie War, because Fox News tells you one led to the other, but I don't agree. The government didn't let everybody out of prison because of me, it was because they ran out of money. I mean, it's sick, right? You have to ask, why did we spend so much money on prisons if it was money we didn't have? So you expect all these cats to be back on the streets and now they become law abiding citizens, when the whole world is going to hell? You blame them for what happened? What did we teach them in prison? How being in a gang is key to survival. How many zombies were created during the financial crisis, you want to blame the prisoners for that, too? Just the opposite. 'Five billion fines, no one doing time.' What about the opioid crisis? 'Five billion fines, no one doing time.' How many zombies were created then? All this before the war, the plague, the famine. Time to stop pointing fingers. If this taught me one thing, when towers fall and seas rise, we have to come together. When the challenge is survival, that's humanity. Our problems begin when we try to exclude someone from being part of the human experience. Any attempt to divide the human race, along any lines, has always ended badly, the result misery, injustices and hatred on both sides of the line. The best part of humanity knows no division. We're happiest when we're together. This is Sensi Star, signing off, check my next single, 'You, Me, Under the Old Tree,' out for Valentine's Day, and who knows, maybe next time I see you, it will be live!"

FRANKFORDSTEIN

by Bertram Montiekowicz

YOU SEEN A ZOMBIE, REALLY?

Oh, under the El? Big deal.

The zombie invasion's already over, you missed it.

Last night, while you were sleeping, a zombie crept down your street, checked to see if your car door was unlocked, peeked in your window, licked its lips.

I'm talking about 1977, a little different then.

I wasn't even from Frankford, what was I doing here? How did I end up getting stuck here the rest of my life?

I don't need to tell you why a 17 year old boy might act irrationally, it was "my girlfriend."

If she was here with me under the El while I'm telling you the story, she might admit she was my girlfriend, or she might say 'bullshit.'

At 15, how could she be anyone's anything? I still call her my girl.

Anyone familiar with the law understands my dangerous situation, falling for a freshman with my 18th birthday looming. One day, I'm dreaming of losing my virginity, the next it's a cardinal offense. I had no idea what we were supposed to do as a couple, and nothing ever happened between us. As she was no virgin, she had total control.

When she called I came running, and that meant taking the bus to Frankford, riding the El from one end of Filthadelfia to the other.

To prove how much I didn't belong, had neither proper attitude nor attire, my girl would suddenly exit the car, flee down the stairs, out through the spinning metal gate, into some of the most interesting neighborhoods this country has ever seen.

I begged her to stop running. I was frustrated, in every sense of the word. We were spending a lot of time together but there was no progress. It was like she needed to be with me but hated every moment we were together. My memories are bathed in red.

You say you're going to publish this, right?

Well, I have to say a little bit about Frankford. I know, nobody cares, but what if you have readers from Canada? They need to know how there was a zombie in Frankford, a real one.

Let's go back to the original day.

Imagine, right where we're at, Frankford was like the little town outside Philadelphia, and Philadelphia was the jewel of the Empire, proof civilization could be brought to savage lands, and done in peace.

Think of it this way. If you were in Philly and headed north, or in New York heading south, you had to go through Frankford. There was no other way to do it. They called it the King's Highway. I know, it's hard to believe. They put the El right over it. Like most of the King's Highway, Frankford Ave got its start as an Indian footpath. So think about that, people walking by for ten thousand years, maybe more, they have no idea because the Indians, you know, they would have never thought of building something like the El, they didn't see it as their place to scar the earth forever.

     FRANKFORDSTEIN

I get it, nobody gives a shit. Just tell them to look it up.

Sam Adams and John Adams, when they were coming down for the Revolution, you know, the third of July or whatever it was, right before we declared independence, of course they stayed the night in Frankford. They were met for drinks by Benjamin Rush and some of the other locals. The Philadelphians convinced the Massachusetts Delegation to let the Virginians take the lead, let Washington command the army, Jefferson write the official document, let them do everything. Make it seem like it was all their idea. It worked like a charm. Think of that, right where you're sitting America is born, not at Independence Hall, but a bar in Frankford. I'm telling you, the Jolly Post was right there, where the Wawa is.

Think of it like Brooklyn, Frankford retained its identity, even its wealth, right up until the market crashed. You need money to win an NFL Championship, right? Especially back then. That's why you see mansions on one block, twins on the next, rowhomes, the Frankford capitalists saw themselves as benevolent titans, they wanted to share a community with their workers. Everybody in Frankford thought bringing in the El was going to make them rich, as people would come from around the city to shop here. Then the car came in and that was it. The women of Frankford had clout, though, you have to give them credit. They got the city to put the pillars for the El in the middle of Frankford Ave so there would be less shadows on the shop windows. Best laid plans, right?

So Frankford is the perfect place for someone to sell their soul, it was a buyer's market during the Depression. Frankford was full of ancient American families trapped in their mansions. Generations passed, lavish estates in disrepair.

Face it, though, Frankford was always a failed utopia. The idealists climbed the first hill above the city, and they called their new home Frankford, because it was on the other side of Frankford Creek.

Ah, Frankford Creek. I can still smell it, as it used to be. The name appears on a Dutch map from before the English took over. We'll never know who Frank was. That's how old the name is. The Swedes used the creek to grind grist, that's why the flag of Philadelphia has Sweden's colors, Penn wanted to honor the first residents. Then the Yellow Jackets took the colors from the flag for their uniform.

When this was Indian land, the water was crystal clear. You can still catch carp in Frankford Creek, down by the Arsenal, when the river comes in, guy pulled a seven pounder the other day.

Compare that to the 70s. Reeking trash everywhere. The city didn't have any money for that. Graffiti, not that I'm going to sit here and complain, I destroyed my share of property.

The difference, my father printed get-out-of-jail free cards on his desk downtown.

Liberty, not everybody's ready for it, I know I wasn't.

My girl had simply seized her own liberty, like the Frankford revolutionaries of yore.

Overnight it seemed, Frankford went from this place I never heard of to one with extreme relevance. My life had been turned upside down.

Since most days she wished I wasn't by her side, there would be these tests, to see what extreme I would go to. I thought she wanted me to prove my love.

Give her credit, though, my girl always had her ear to the ground.

You want a joint, right, there's nothing wrong with that, we've been smoking plants since the dawn of time. I don't expect any argument from you guys on that one. But when you're just a kid, and you smoke a joint, and it's no big deal, you lose faith in the government.

What's next? How about some coke? Can't you just sell to support your habit? It happens that quick.

The things I seen, sure that night stands alone, but there's a lot of bizarre shit under this El.

Maybe the zombies figured out how to blend in, you didn't think about that one, did you?

Go over and ask him. How about if it was late at night, you want to go talk to him? Dude gets on the El, covered with dirt, stains that might be blood. You going to say, 'Yo, man, what's up? You really alive?'

Somehow my girl learned there was a haunted house in Frankford.

The old heads from R&W, Oxford Circle, they'll remember what I'm talking about.

It was right on The Boulevard, by Sears, before they brought it down... you remember the old Sears tower, don't you? The faces on the clock, when you were coming up on it, looked like this huge owl, staring down.

It was the older kids who set up the haunted house. The younger kids, it's like, do you dare go in, you're breaking the law. There were strange images painted on the walls, patrons added their own contribution. You didn't know who was around the next corner. Could be anybody.

What did it smell like in the haunted house?

Dirt weed and wet foundation. How's that?

Outside the haunted house, when we stepped off the R bus, there were a couple younger kids loitering, you could see they were scared to go in. These kids were only a couple years younger, but they looked like little boys to me. I didn't think about it then, but they were probably my girlfriend's age.

She walked right into the abandoned house without a moment's hesitation, and I did the same.

Now, I wish I could tell you exactly every detail, but I was so pissed about everything that had transpired over the previous 24 hours. Where to begin, what started it. Like I said, I have trouble remembering. Everything felt wrong. I was supposed to be looking at colleges and getting ready for that, and look what I was doing.

This particular day, I think it was a Thursday, we had both simply walked out of school after second period. We had a busy day planned.

The haunted house was completely empty. We went from one end to the other without incident and she backtracked, poking into dark corners.

"It's stupid," she said.

She erupted into a scream, it sounded like I had stabbed her. Then she tried to lock me in. I heard a ruckus in the street, had to climb out the back window, jog down The Boulevard to catch up with her. She's stomping away and the traffic is beeping like we're in New York.

What an ass I was, but it's the things you do for love. I mean it was love, right, pure love? Why else act like I had surrendered control of my very self.

Like I said, nothing ever happened between us, other than a lot of extreme talk. Our relationship was an all or nothing bet: either we were going to spend the rest of our lives together, or we wouldn't be able to spend another second.

My father had gambled away anything that might become an inheritance, but my superficially steady home life convinced my girl, perhaps on an instinctive level, that I might cut it as a father. I'm sure my kids will say she was dead wrong on that one, but they never knew me then, before I lost her.

I keep trying to convince myself, maybe she rejected me for my own good. Sometimes selfish people harbor a low opinion of themselves, and repel someone they actually like. She knew if we

     FRANKFORDSTEIN

stayed together it would be like subjecting me to a lifetime of misery. I was ready for that and more.

Frankford Creek still drips down to the Delaware, it's never going away. Think about what it's seen.

My girl's eyes are drawn to the black water. She dips her head dangerously over the bridge. The creek is silent, reflecting the bright moonlight with the barest shimmer. I know what's next, we're going to be climbing down into this muddy polluted gulch.

Back in Sam Adams' day if you bought land next to the creek it gave you the right to dump whatever you wanted.

The dye works was right there; some days the creek was blue, purple, red, but the odor was always the same, a magnet for mosquitoes, who floated dead like everything else.

No smartphones, few cameras, how many images do we have of street life after the sun sets? It might as well be an Alien world, one we'll never see again.

My girl expected and found a pathway on the other end of the bridge, grass worn by human feet. The fence had been snapped free and pushed open. She ducked through into complete darkness, down the slope and around the foliage, out of sight.

Angrier now, the endless nature of the escapade, just wishing she would stop making me chase, I called.

I yelled her name, I don't know what else, commands, requests, begs. I could hear people scurrying from our trespass, I could sense them, I knew they were there because they were afraid.

Inside the homes we passed shades bent, doors cracked. We were the lunatics. Some places people yell in the street more often than others. You have to understand, cops are underpaid and overworked.

The full moon reached its apex. I could see her for a moment on the dirt path ahead. She ran on tip toe, the wood nymph from a fairy tale, here to enchant, cause chaos, mischief. I followed.

Soon we were in a stranger setting still, the creek, shrunken, rerouted by man with backbreaking labor, channeled between the tall walls of two dead warehouses, whose black eyes watched from broken windows, kids out to prove they could aim, they didn't care. I was one of them. We destroyed everything we could lay our hands on.

There were little walkways behind the warehouses, a concrete bank. Beyond the warehouse valley loomed a bridge over the creek, I assumed it was Large Street. She ran ahead as I screamed and threw rocks. It seemed we were alone.

Before the tunnel she paused for a playful look, no fear, just eager to relish, and then the black mouth swallowed her whole.

Something in my screech, I didn't think there was another level, maybe it was my tears, unrecognizable as a feature of anger; the vocal chords can only take so much; perhaps inside the tunnel the acoustics changed, her harmonies, I'll never be able to explain her.

I mean, you can kind of guess the kind of life she had up until now, but she was smart. We were in the same school, she through academic achievement against all odds, teachers and counselors legally bound to provide protection, like parents should be, and me because of my father's Rolodex.

I went on to graduate in the top 90% of my class, she had entered her final hour.

Ah man, why did I even agree to do this.

Can't you just run with that? I'm done. Well what are you going to do with this? As soon as that bus comes I'm out of here.

Whatever. I'm not sure why this is so important to you. I don't care. Whatever.

Where were we, oh yeah, lost.

I thought we were under the bridge formed by Large Street, but when I went back years later, you know, that sick way they catch all the criminals; and why, because you're fucked up, you can't stop

FRANKFORDSTEIN

thinking about the crime. They call it PTSD but didn't she have it already before the zombie got her?

It was like she passed it to me, because I couldn't tell anyone what I seen, nobody. There's treatments today but this was '77, the guys from 'Nam couldn't get help, and look what they went through.

It's no surprise criminals return to the scene, but for me, I just lied and lied. I played dumb, it was a role I knew well. Her body would never show up, I knew that much. I had to keep the secret as long as my father lived, I owed it to him. I couldn't give in to the temptation, risk coming face to face with the local cops who could tell I was full of shit, who let it go for the sake of their career.

The witnesses all had the same story, some big scary looking dude chasing a young girl, but it couldn't have been me right? My story was I got tired of chasing. I never had to go downtown, face a jury. I could not recall where I was the last time I seen her, that much was true. I found my way home, jumped the El; when you're the zombie, nobody says shit to you.

But that's not what happened.

She came out of the tunnel and gave me a prolonged hug.

Maybe that was my moment, and I let my petty feelings get in the way. Maybe if I had any maturity she wouldn't have died, maybe we could have consummated our relationship while it was still legal, and she wasn't hoping to get knocked up, as my father routinely prophesied.

Instead she ripped free, ran back alongside the concrete bank, between the abandoned warehouses, and disappeared inside. The moonlight revealed her shadow moving fast. I had to follow.

She was fearless, and crossed the length of the warehouse without incident, while I got a piece of broken glass stuck in my boot.

I dared not stop to get it out as I didn't want to lose sight of her. The warehouse had no front at all, so she simply stepped into a new street, which was well lit. I caught up and the broken glass in my boot screeched across the pavement. I tried to get it out but cut my finger good, it kept bleeding, I tried wiping it on my shirt.

She said, "Don't drink too much of your own blood."

My girl, what was she? She never worried if I was in pursuit, just walked away. Somehow, I knew where she was headed.

I looked up and down the street, as far as I could see, trying to get my bearings, knowing how this ends, not with a zombie, but back on the El, that lasting monument, a ticket out, and at school she skimmed tokens from her criminal network, she had an endless supply.

Back then you couldn't rely on street signs and there weren't any, even on the corner.

Facing our warehouse across the street, its twin, this one still in operation. There was a blue and yellow sign on the front. It was locked up good and tight, she checked. We climbed up onto the train tracks, which ran behind the warehouse. There was a huge sign painted on the brick wall for the original business, but the white letters were fading, I forget what it was, an obsolete part for a machine no one uses anymore, J.B. Brisker & Sons, something like that. There were more tracks running through the neighborhood, but this one only carried freight. While my girl tried the windows I stared at the sign: an illegible ad for a useless product, in a place where there was no one left to read it.

The sky was gray, and the light pollution made it hard to see much further than I could from the street below. I hoped to determine where we were in relation to Center City, but remember back then you weren't allowed to build over the top of Billy Penn's head.

I heard the El, but wasn't sure if it was coming or going.

     FRANKFORDSTEIN

We were surely lost but this was nothing new for her.

With the determination of a triathlete she kept going, back down the other side of the tracks, across the quiet street, which bent around a turn to the right, and split a park to the left.

These old train tracks were extracted years later, the trestles removed, too many shadows in Frankford already; that's one of the reasons I can't find where we were. After losing her I just kept listening for the El, and by dawn, I found my way to Church Street Station, coming up from the river, which doesn't make any sense because we started out on the other side of The Boulevard.

She walked fast but was running out of gas.

Where the rowhomes started, not far from the shadow of the trestle, she found a little cubby hole with a steep set of stairs leading into darkness. The cubby was shaped on either side with cinderblock. The construction looked like a do-it-yourself job, a way to access the second floor from the street, probably one of these guys renting a room illegally.

She asked, "Do you love me or the idea of me?"

I said, "What the fuck is the difference."

We were side by side on different steps, huddled in the shadows. She opened a pack of Marlboro Lights and I could see she was down to her wish cigarette. She lit it and quickly blew a small exhale.

She said, "I think you love the idea of me. When we're together I feel like... two dimensional, I don't really exist, I'm only here as an extension of you, like you invented me for some purpose, and I'm not sure why, I'll never know. And then you get mad as soon as I'm not exactly what you imagined I should be, when I don't do exactly what you think I was created to do. You act like I'm in a movie about you."

I said, "I don't understand half the shit you say."

"Well, listen closely, I know your little letter, with the poem, I know you didn't write it, they're just lyrics from a song."

"I never said I wrote it."

"Yeah, you just wrote it."

"Next time I'll put footnotes."

"Don't be a dick."

"So what if I didn't write it. So what? It doesn't change what I said: everything is just Dust in the Wind."

She looked away, took a long drag on the cigarette, blew it out, offered it to me. I refused.

She asked, "What if you had to actually write something original? What if, you know, you had to write about what we're doing now, what would you say about me? Would you say I was beautiful, that I captured your heart? Will you tell them how you chased me?" She paused for effect. "Will you tell them how you slapped me?"

"I never fucking slapped you."

"You're such a liar Chuck! Who are you even lying to? There's just you and me here."

We heard a shuffling behind us, atop the dark stairs. She turned with me, but it must have been the wind swirling leaves in the street, echoes.

Hissing, I said, "I told you I was sorry, it was an accident, I raised my hand—" she cut me off so efficiently when our faces were this close.

"Yeah, that's why they call it a slap."

"I didn't know you were going to stand up at exactly that moment! You won't forgive me but I did not mean to hit you. It was just, like I said, I shouldn't have raised my hand."

She watched me for a second before standing. "Yeah, no shit."

She broke free the burning end from the cigarette and tucked the remainder into her empty pack. Rigid, she walked slowly this time, turning to the left, not the way we came, always in search of something new. I walked by her side in silence, wondering if this was the night. Should I try to hold her hand? Where do you start?

We stumbled into an old part of Frankford. There were cobblestones in the tight street and a curb formed by long slabs of gray granite. It was expensive to build streets this way, but they worked well for horses, carts, how the rich got around with their goods. Now there were cars parked with two tires on the pavement in front of us, fearful of getting their mirror clipped. Past the cars I could see a row of trees growing out of the sidewalk on both sides of the street. The houses across the street were invisible, there must have been at least ten steps separating them from the sidewalk, and each had some kind of gate or wall, rows of bushes. Nothing stirred.

The city hadn't gotten around to updating the street lights, they held an orange glow. I heard the El again, and when I tilted my head a mist came up the block, but it had to be there the whole time, right? We were getting closer to the orange light, and that made it seem like the mist came rolling down the block. When I looked behind us, the mist already obscured our path. The full moon shining through rendered even the orange light into shades of black and white.

She gave me a glance, smiling. She asked, "Did you think this was going to happen?"

A few hours before I invited her over for dinner with the family for the first time, man what a mistake. The conversation between her and my parents, what was I thinking?

She couldn't believe I wouldn't eat the fat on my mother's roast pork, and when I was done, she reached over and ate the wormy pieces I had separated from the meat. When I asked her why she said she liked to see me squirm.

We took a few steps and I saw a black metal fence bent into points. Fingers of dead brown vines reached out, like they were trying to claw themselves free. The leaves piled up, I couldn't see what the fence held. Aligned with the beginning of the fence, the pavement changed from a regular cheap concrete pad into a pattern of small interlocking red brick. It looked like a zipper to me. So many red bricks in this city, but these were lighter in color, perhaps fired just for this job. I followed my feet. The bricks were worn, some were missing, especially where the tree roots bulged the brickwork out of the earth. The pattern became an abstraction, I felt dizzy. A zipper with so many missing teeth could never work.

She backhanded me in the chest, kindly. I looked up, past her, we were next to a cemetery. The black fence had rusted out, you could see where kids were sneaking in. I figured for sure we would enter, but she walked on.

The weeds were overgrown, the grave markers carved from thin white stone, weathered by time, such that you couldn't read the names. There were taller markers, some had little symbols, obscured by the mist.

Maybe she was the type to take my virginity in a graveyard?

I caught up with her at the cemetery gate.

She lifted her hood. I knew this to be a queue. Whenever she wanted to commit a crime, up went the hood. She pulled open the cemetery gate and it didn't make a sound. The familiar red brick path continued, straight into the mist, faded white gravestones to either side. Inside the gate the stones were less worn, and the zipper pattern complete, but it still made me dizzy.

I noticed she had an envelope in her hand, like she was trying to read something in the dim light without me seeing what it was. I looked over her shoulder but she hid it and moved off. After that, I acted like I wasn't trying to see what she was reading. I thought it might be a diagram of some kind. She had more than one.

     FRANKFORDSTEIN

I could never find the cemetery again after that night. It must have been absorbed by another cemetery. Sometimes they have to move the bodies, there's tombstones in the Wissahickon you can see at low tide, they dumped the corpses in a mass grave. Who cares, right? If there's nobody from the history books, no one left to remember the dead, what do you do with an old cemetery? Could be real estate.

So much of the landscape changed since 77, gentrification, renewal, repurposing. Back then abandoned houses stared from every block, the older kids used them to stash contraband, as headquarters. Only later did they become crack houses. The city cleared entire blocks so businesses could get tax breaks.

When I look at Google Maps, we must have been behind Friends Hospital.

You'd be surprised how many green spaces there are in Frankford, and that's the biggest, mostly because of the cemeteries.

A couple blocks from where we're at right now is the only intersection in the country with a different cemetery on every corner. People have been dying in Frankford for a long time.

We kept walking. It seemed like nothing changed, we were on a conveyor belt in a nightmare. The mist had a wetness, I smelled dead leaves burning. There was a gunshot in the distance, or maybe it was a broken down car backfiring. Nearby dogs offered a chorus of replies.

Then, looming in front of us, this black figure.

I froze as my girl continued forward, stood below, half its height. She bent her head. I took a step forward, into the shadow, to see a statuesque tombstone, some memorial to a great man. The bearded statue had its right hand over the heart, fingertips hidden by the fold of a military jacket. The plaque beneath the soldier's boots had a number of details, and my girl flicked her lighter, illuminating her agile mind.

She said, "Wow. I have to say, I'm amazed. I could have never guessed in a million years this would work, and yet, here he is,

Colonel Henry Stelter, just like you said. Caught Yellow Fever and died alongside most of his entourage. You see how they do it. They don't commemorate why he came to Philadelphia in the first place. No mention of the rich Philadelphians who wanted to finance his exploits in Mexico in exchange for Spanish land. They just leave that part out."

I said, "Very interesting."

She gave me a look. "You're in a weird mood. It's like you're not even there."

"Well you act like I'm supposed to know who you're talking about."

Her look devolved into a smile; I guess she thought I was kidding.

We heard a sound from behind the closest tombstone and instinctively froze.

The mist shivered in silence, then a rat jumped onto the red brick path. I almost shit myself. These city rats, they're large, unafraid. It hissed at us before darting out of sight. My girl, she had to react, a burst of hilarity that echoed against the metal statue. She clamped one hand to her mouth and let her eyes do the laughing.

When the moment passed, she danced around the statue, away from the street lights, into the old soldier's shadow. I had the sense I would never see her again, and vaulted to remain by her side.

After a few paces she stopped and I turned to see what caught her attention. There, to our right, against the back corner of the cemetery, the wrought iron fence reappeared, sturdier here, blacker. A row of small trees grew on either side, making it impossible to know what lay beyond. She stepped over the graves, carefully, I knew she had been through too many funerals, too many close deaths. That's why, I think, she never knew who to trust.

When I looked up there was a black gate in the wrought iron fence. The gate opened of its own accord, but it was her, right, it had to be, kicking it, so swiftly and silently, to me it was another dark portal, and those who went beyond were doomed never to return.

She walked through and I could not let her go alone.

I couldn't hear traffic anymore.

She paused, I hoped afraid, but it was just for a moment, to let her eyes adjust. The foliage grew close above our heads, weeds were under our feet. To the left of the path, along a small ridge, three large stones were piled into a set of stairs. The stones had specks of mica reflecting the moonlight in a thousand places.

She tip-toed up the sparkling steps. A fence laced with trench warfare barbed wire ran along the ridge, but there was a chain link gate facing the old stone stairs. An open padlock hung from the loop. She simply lifted it and the latch to pull the gate open. She dove through the fronds and disappeared. I could hear her crunching away, and pressed through the brush after her.

Our feet found asphalt, which was reassuring, but soon we switched to dirt, keeping the security fence to our right and an open field shrouded by mist on our left. The clouds were drifting in and out, shafts of moonlight chasing shadows. I kept expecting something to appear, as if in a spotlight.

The dirt path curved around the property but my girl headed straight over a patch of grass, towards an old wall, maybe about eight feet up, with a wider lintel fastened on top for support. You could see the wall was ancient, made from stones they found lying on the ground, with concrete between. Maybe a hundred years ago someone covered the wall with plaster, but large sections had fallen off, revealing the original construction. The security fence with the barbed wire ended where it met the old wall.

"Give me a boost," she said. I laced my fingers together and she added her tiny foot. When I stood she elevated with me, grabbing the lintel and pulling herself the rest of the way. She laid on the flat stone for a moment before clambering onto the roof of a shed built against the wall on the other side. I jumped and pulled myself over, landing with a thud.

"Where the hell are we going?"

"This was all your idea."

"What are you talking about?"

"You said you wanted to go to a haunted house, well, here we are."

I turned to see an old house looming, dark, with those ornate roofs, eaves twisting shadows in the moonlight. I figured it must be an old church, so close to the cemetery, I didn't learn until later the cemeteries came first, and the churches were erected to honor the dead, and not the other way around.

Then I thought maybe the whole deal was part of the old mental institution. The founders of Friends Hospital, back in the 1800s, would need their own cemetery. If that was the case we were surrounded by the graves of the country's first mental patients, the ones who never made it out. You'd think they'd keep the place in better shape.

More likely this was some old religion from a bygone day, and there's only a handful of adherents left, a utopian cult that fled Europe and went extinct in Frankford.

None of this would have surprised me at the time, but my girl walked up to the front door like she was coming home from school.

School, I thought, mere hours away; we both hated it, she would never have to go again.

At her numerous tributes I stood alone, my fingers clenched around a feeble bouquet, which had also been cut down too soon for the wrong reason.

My peers didn't need an official investigation to find me guilty. Everyone knew I would never leave her side while she breathed. At the very least, I knew her fate and refused to reveal it, just let them all keep searching and hoping because it was the only way to save my own skin.

The old house seemed deserted. She tested every opening, finding one in the old storm doors that went straight down into the basement. A rusted chain held the doors closed. Designed for a time when people didn't rob each other, the chain's presence likely indicated there was no other lock.

She said, "I can't believe you're not strong enough to break that chain."

I grabbed the door with a jerk.

She said, "Come on, put your back into it!"

I kept pulling, and when the rusted link sagged it gave me the encouragement I needed to snap it. The door opened, banged with a clang, and she laughed.

A big dog barked, somewhere to our left, there must be houses behind the cemetery, or maybe an auto lot, the kind of place that would leave a dog out in the middle of the night. A few smaller dogs replied. The sound echoed for a moment, then it was quiet.

She figured it would be easy to explore the basement, but my shadow blocked the moonlight. I didn't realize until she went down hard, with a thud. When I stepped to the side the white moon poured back into the cellar. I could see her lying there. She turned to me, laughing before dusting herself off.

She said, "I think I hit my head."

I met her at the bottom of the stairs and she lowered the hood so I could confirm her suspicions. She asked, "What excuse should I use for this one?"

"Me? What did I do?"

"You're going to stand there and say you didn't cause this?"

We turned to a noise upstairs in the house. I said, "Someone's here."

"Charles." She knew I hated being called Charles. Even Chas would have been better. And yes, I know what Poe had to say about guys named Charles.

"There's no mailbox, Charles, no wires. You didn't notice?"

I hadn't. I liked the idea of staying close to the cellar door, in the moonlight.

I asked, "What is all this shit?"

She said, "Shit it is."

Her deft fingers were rifling, more shopper than thief. Spores of old mold pocked the boxes, as if the basement had flooded and no one did anything about it. That's what it smelled like anyway. She pulled a weird metal utensil from a box and showed it to me. Maybe it was an egg beater.

Then we heard it.

"What the hell was that?" This time it was me again.

She had a finger to her lips.

I said, "That wasn't a footstep."

"Let's go see."

"Why?"

"I want to see what kind of person would live in a place like this."

"Why?"

"The depths, right? The depths of the human soul. That's what we're here for right, breaking into houses, suffering at school like some kind of prisoner, everywhere you go in this filthy city." I noticed she didn't say home because it wasn't something we shared; I was quite content, the food was well prepared and timely. Her conclusion was apt. "I'm so sick of watching old people line up on election day to decide my future."

Regardlessly, as my mother would say, my love for this person caused me to set aside everything everyone had ever given me, permanently, I assumed.

And now here we were, breaking and entering.

A light came on, not in the basement, but spilling from upstairs. The door to the basement must have been open. The basement stairs were closeby, in the center of the house. We heard the sound again and I knew what it was, a wheelchair.

"Who's down there?" An old lady's voice.

In a whisper, my girl said, "Come on, let's go."

She strode confidently into the play of light from upstairs, smiling.

The old lady asked, "What do you think you are, some kind of witch?"

It was the heavy make-up, my girl got it a lot. By now the young witch was halfway there.

The old lady's voice became more shrill. "What are you doing in my house?"

"I'm lost." My girl stopped.

I held my position, unsure.

How had her previous boyfriends responded when the caper went wrong? And why would I act as they did, if they became previous boyfriends? I felt like I needed to do something different, but all I could do was stare like a man paralyzed. I tried to picture the old lady in the wheelchair as she held my girl in her gaze but all I see is the same mist from the street.

The old lady, well, you can imagine, she lost it, shouting, get out of my house, man I couldn't take it, but my girl smiled. Eventually the old lady had to catch her breath.

That's when my girl said, "I just need a couple bucks, you know, for the El."

The old lady gathered herself. "You crook, get out of my house! You think you're a witch! I was a witch long before you went to Claire's for dark eye shadow. You're some kind of rent-a-witch, you wouldn't know how to cast a spell if the book was opened and the candles were lit. There's nothing magical about you, you're just sick, and you try to cover it up, cake over the horror, with horror. Now get out of my house. You need a couple bucks? Well here, take this."

There was a pause, I assumed the old lady was reaching into her pocket. She threw something down the steps. I couldn't see what it was but my girl caught it against herself, backed away, until she hit the bottom, turned, kept moving, right past me.

In that weird light, I swear I saw eyes, looking at me, whatever the old lady threw, as it flashed down the steps, they weren't human eyes, they had slits for pupils, like a snake, or the Sears tower when the clock strikes midnight.

We made our way from the house, used the shed to get back over the wall, near the sparkling stone staircase where my girl found a bright patch of clearing. She examined the haul, impressed. It was a necklace, and the chain might have been silver.

Maybe the pause had been the old lady removing it from her own throat.

The fob was odd, like a little box, and my girl kept messing with it until she got it open.

Inside was a powder, I assumed it was the remains of someone from a crematorium, but my girl, her face lit up, she loved solving puzzles.

I don't know what she was doing, but she snorted the powder up her nose, like, it was spasmodic, and she looked at me, wide-eyed, I don't know what she expected. My look of surprise set her off laughing. She was laughing so loud I looked back at the house and I swear, through the trees, there was a light, and I could see the old lady's silhouette in the window, her shadow had a wavy line coming out of it, and I knew she was on the phone. She must be calling the cops. We had to get out of there. I turned to my girl in the failing moonlight. The humor had gone out of the moment but she liked to laugh, and could keep herself laughing. The laugh's contrived nature, and its fervor, made her sound mad. She liked to get this fake laugh going, and I just wanted it to stop.

I almost had to drag her back the way we came, but at the black gate into the old cemetery, she dug in her heels. Her laughter stopped suddenly as we crossed the threshold. She seemed pissed I had dragged her into a cemetery while she was laughing, even if it was fake. She stared at me a long time with this horrible look of pity.

I remember her face, around the nostrils, splotches of red. I could tell she was ashamed. She looked teary eyed, insane, and tried to wipe the powdery residue from her face.

With a solemn air she returned to the old man's statue.

It was like we were starting all over again.

She flicked her lighter at the tombstones, one at a time, patiently, as I stood watching, numb.

She said, "Found him."

She fell down to the ground in front of the tombstone and started dragging at the grass with her hands. It was futile. I didn't know what to say. The mist hung low over the cemetery.

She looked up at me. "Aren't you going to help?"

"No, I'm not going to help. What are you fucking nuts?"

"Get a tool, there's got to be something, maybe a stone even, we just got to break the surface. How deep can these old graves be? There's erosion right?"

"We're graverobbers now?"

She dug the necklace out and threw it at me, and there were those slit eyes again, looking right through me.

I convinced myself it was a trick of the moonlight; we can desecrate the dead, there's no afterlife.

I looked at the inscription inside the metal box on the necklace.

JEZEBEL — NEVER FORGET ME
R. H. M. 1807

She paused, watching me. I leaned down, collected some of the loose dirt with my free hand and smeared it into the depressions on the white tombstone, where the clay glowed red.

ROBERT HAMILTON MOORE 1793 — 1813

In the same font, but smaller so it fit across the width of the stone, it said,

BORN: BATON ROUGE

Beneath, another inscription had been stripped away with several blows from a sharp chisel.

We were both on the ground beside the grave.

My review nearly complete, I heard her digging again, more tentatively. I turned when she whelped. She was staring at her fingernail.

I asked, "Did you hurt yourself?"

She shot me that look. She hated to say "of course," but always felt like saying it. "You could be helping. I'm sure there's something we can use."

I got to my feet, looped the silver chain around my neck, and began my search.

Lunging this way and that from the grave, deeper into the mist, alone among the tombstones, trying to keep my bearings, and then there it was on the ground at my feet: a paving stone in the shape of a pentagon. I pulled it free. It was heavy and fit nicely in my hands.

I rushed back and she was sitting there, beside the grave, ready to dig.

Even after I sank the pointed stone into the ground and began peeling away the earth, her little hands were darting here and there, clearing the pile or lifting a clump that tumbled into the hole.

I had a nice pit going, and she was right there beside me.

Wait, did you guys feel that, like a chill? You didn't feel that? It was like the breeze that warns you winter is near. I feel like she's sitting beside me again.

She said, "You're telling the story all wrong. You act like all the experiences we shared happened on the same day."

I kept digging. "What are you talking about?"

"You, you're fucked up."

"Stop saying that!"

She paused, squinting. "Did you take more acid?"

"No! How could you ask me that, after what happened last time. I told you I was done."

"But you had some left."

"I flushed it."

"You're such a liar."

"Me? You're the one who gave it to me."

"Fuck you Chuck! You asked me to get it for you! You want to blame me for everything, I'm the victim here!"

In the quiet, I sank the point of the heavy stone deeper and deeper into the ground.

She said, "I heard you could have flashbacks."

"What?"

"Like, your mind is, I don't know, broken."

"I doubt that."

"You made it seem like we arrived here randomly, but you wanted to come here. It was your idea to dig the grave. You said you had a vision while you were tripping. You put clues into little envelopes and told me to open them in order. There's only one left."

She laid the letters beside the grave like a fortune teller. They had my handwriting on them.

"Why do you gotta fuck with me like this?"

She said, "You were going to tell the story all wrong."

Angry, I asked, "What about the old lady in the wheelchair?"

"Aunt Mary?"

"Mary." I touched the fob on the chain, trying to remember. It wasn't a square box, but a flat circle. "What about the witch, in the haunted house? You're going to say it never happened?"

"What are you talking about?"

"Just now! The old lady, you're going to say we didn't rob an old lady? We didn't break into her basement and rob her?"

"That was like, two weeks ago."

"And she gives you the name of the person we're supposed to dig up?"

"She gave me two half dollars."

"She threw them down the steps."

"Yeah, you were standing right there."

Frothing almost I ripped the chain from my neck. "This chain, where'd you get the chain?"

"You gave it to me!"

"Well where did I get it from?"

She wanted to answer but took a second to appreciate how absurd I sounded.

Instead she made a sound of disgust. "Where did you get it from. You never told me! What's wrong with you?"

Icy cold, my mouth went dry.

I asked, "Why am I digging this grave?"

She watched me carefully. "You really can't remember?"

"Godammit, what did I say!"

She took a deep breath. "You said I could stop worrying about America, that everything was going to be ok, you knew how to finish what Manson started. You figured out how to bring on Helter Skelter, the race war. All you had to do was resurrect one of these slaveholders, parade him around, let him do the talking. Everybody would see how good white people used to have it, and it would be like the good ol' days." She pointed at the old soldier's statue with her thumb. "Colonel Henry Stelter's spirit sought you out while you were tripping. That was the first thing you said when you went into a trance, 'Helter Skelter, Hitler Shelter, Henry Stelter.' His plantation was in Louisiana, but he's buried here in Frankford, that's why he can't rest. You're digging the grave of the zombie Stelter brought with him from down south. The Colonel caught his slaves practicing voodoo, and so he ordered them to summon a zombie to protect him on the road, while he was in Philadelphia. It was the Colonel who told you to dig up the zombie first. He said it will be strong enough to knock over his statue. It's the only way to get him out. Man you were tripping hard. You were writing, drawing, sealing envelopes, ripping them up. You were crying, you locked yourself in the bathroom. When you came out you gave me the envelopes, and you said, never tell me about these, and open them in the right order, you'll know when."

For a moment everything was clear: there were two necklaces and two old ladies; my girl wore her mother's remains around her neck; what she snorted was cocaine the night I caught her with Jimmy Piscarcek's older brother, and nobody could understand why I had to kick his ass, and when his brother jumped in, it was like a movie, with the shelves getting knocked over, broken glass. Dudes grabbing anything for a weapon.

When I returned from suspension with one brother hospitalized and the other traumatized, it marked the end of my long career of fighting at school, sixty-one bouts in all. Until then everyone wanted to try their luck against the big guy, especially one who seemed a little slow. I was happy to oblige; I was a monster long before my girl went missing.

Clarity.

We had robbed an old lady of some change. We broke into the basement, the old lady panicked, threw us the money. Aunt Mary was the one in the wheelchair, and she was nobody's aunt. We only met her like a month ago.

Mary's ancestor took the money he was going to give Stelter and set up a society, designed to preserve tradition. Now only she remained, the last of a dying breed, a religion with no adherents.

Aunt Mary, after she was dead and gone, so would die her ancestors' dream of returning the white man to his rightful place.

Mary found her answer in the occult, lured my girl in, called her a rent-a-witch. After that, it was like my girl became Mary's disciple. She had to do everything the old witch said, including putting me under a spell.

Instead of eye of newt they just used LSD. I proved susceptible to trance, easy to control, the perfect zombie in every way. When she was done Mary erased herself from my memory. I still couldn't tell you what she looked like.

Does that make me innocent, if my will had been taken? Wouldn't that make all lovers innocent? Is that love, sharing every passion our partner espouses, mindlessly?

I never even asked my girl how she ended up so prejudiced against black people.

Now, they always assume the big guy is a dummy, but in between being poisoned by these witches, I learned a little bit about the kind of evil forces I was up against.

They had to trust what I said about the vision.

I had my own game running.

My final letter was written in my own blood, a dead language.

I said, "Whatever you do, don't open that envelope."

She laughed. "All of a sudden you remember everything. Well, the letters have gotten us this far, and you said to ignore you."

"Do not ignore me."

We stared at each other across the open grave and I lost myself in her eyes.

Wistful, I asked, "Why'd you have to die like that?"

At first she laughed. "Now you're creeping me out." Then she grew more serious. "Is there something you haven't told me?"

That's when we heard it, a murmur, a tread, approaching, an unnaturally large shadow pushing through the moonlight mist in the old graveyard.

We saw it was two black guys, twice our age, high and drunk, their heads whispering close. The older man had rounded features, his friend was a little younger, slimmer. They watched us carefully as they continued on their way, which led them closeby.

Me and my girl stood together in front of the half dug grave. The large paving stone dangled from my fingertips, and the older man turned from the pointed rock to my square head with cautious optimism, as despite my size, I was clearly young.

They stopped at a comfortable distance, without departing from their route. The older man asked, "What are you kids doing out here?"

She said, "He's my brother." She grabbed my free arm and hung from it. "He's a little crazy."

The older man glanced at our work. Smile intact, he asked, "You robbing a grave now?"

She spoke again. "This guy is loaded, we'll cut you in if you help us dig him out."

The two men bent their heads togethers again, a quick whisper.

The younger man said, "How about this, we'll keep lookout, you dig."

It seemed like a fair deal to me and I went back to work, sinking the heavy stone into the earth as my girl pushed the dirt to the side. The two men continued to whisper.

She said, "Wait until they see what comes out of this hole."

I actually made it about a foot down, not all the way around. I wanted to make sure the zombie had enough room to crawl out when I broke through the top of its casket. I assumed it would come out quick, after being trapped for so long.

 FRANKFORDSTEIN

My progress hit a snag, it sounded like wood, but it rang like a musical instrument.

The two men approached with interest. Sure enough, in the moonlight I could see something buried, an eyeball staring up at me.

Rather than smashing it again I used my fingers to dig around, and sank my hand into the grave. What came out, I thought was a child's toy. The dirt fell away and you could see bits of cloth and ribbon, it looked hand-made.

When I held it up, the mist peeled away and a beam of moonlight struck a ribbon of red metal that was circled around the doll's throat. Somehow the reflection hit the tombstone, and where I smeared the dirt, the letters glowed.

The old man flinched. He said, "Shit man run that's juju." They took off and the mist swirled in their wake.

The doll showed plenty of care, fashioned from human hair. I stared at it a long time before realizing the sharp metal ribbon had cut me and the doll was soaked with my blood.

My girl paced beside the grave, nervous. "This is bad news. I think we should get out of here."

Music to my ears. I left the paving stone in the hole and started to kick the dirt back in.

"Don't worry about that!" She noticed I was still holding the doll. "What the fuck are you doing, get rid of that thing!"

I turned towards the part of the cemetery we had yet to explore and threw the doll as far as I could into the shadows. It landed with a clatter, I don't know what it hit, it wasn't that heavy, but it knocked something over, one thing into another, seemed like this went on forever. With the second loud clang the big dog was back with a fearsome bark, as if tasked with defending the gates of hell. Every dog in the neighborhood joined in, some were howling and whining.

"What the fuck Charles!"

She ran for the cemetery gate. I was on her trail, but we were in the part of the cemetery that seemed to stretch on endlessly. I knew if I looked down at the pattern of bricks I would get dizzy and lose my way. Gasping, she came to a complete halt.

"They must have known someone would come looking."

"So they use a baby doll to scare us away?"

"It's a totem you idiot. It activated another corpse nearby, the dogs know." The howling intensified. "Perhaps it was a set of corpses."

"A set of corpses?"

She leaned in close so I could hear. "This church celebrated a slaveholder, I'm sure there aren't black people buried here, but sometimes the slaves would be placed in unmarked graves." She scanned the misty graveyard. "If that was the case you'd think they'd be here by now." The dogs reached a crescendo. "Clearly something's alive that shouldn't be, but what could it be?"

She straightened, her able mind addressed each possibility. "Could be."

The dogs lost their fervor and it grew deadly quiet.

I hissed. "It doesn't matter!"

"If I'm right it's not going to matter." She nibbled her lip and nodded. "What if the token is tied to an Indian zombie? Their population was cut in half in the 1800s. That's genocide. For that you need hard hearted men like your colonel. He didn't discriminate between Cherokee, Creek, Choctaw, he wasn't picky, women, children, old men. He told you his soul is in torment, but he never told us why, unless you're keeping something from me. You wouldn't do that would you Charles? Or you do know, and I'm right. There was a church on this same site before they built this one. That happened a lot. It must have been the Swedes, who lived in peace with the Indians. They probably buried their dead in the same place. Church gets built, nobody even knows what they're building on." She seized me for a moment. "What if this was always an Indian cemetery, for tens of thousands of years! Think of how many zombies we're talking about! And you just brought them all to life! It's like a massive mushroom deep beneath the earth. This is even better than I thought. The whole neighborhood is going to get sucked into a sinkhole. You thought the El would always stand." I could see by the look in her eye she had met death in her mind without fear. With the barest smile, she said, "I doubt your father's going to be able to get you out of this one."

The brick pathway undulated, the old gravestones tipped.

I said, "We have to go!"

"No." Her mind was made up. "You already know what's going to happen. It's time to open the final letter."

I slumped. "Please don't, I'm begging you. When I wrote that… I hated you."

"You said you would beg me, that you would make stuff up, that you would do anything to stop me, and that I should read it anyway."

She pulled it out.

"I was tripping!"

I tried to grab the letter but she slapped me. "Don't fucking touch me!" We fell away for the final time. I watched her peel apart the discolored paper, her own blood, which I stole, gumming the seal.

I ran.

Behind me, she read the words, written in my blood. Suscipe me et parcas ei. The sound of her voice made me run faster. She slowly followed down the brick path, repeating the words. Suscipe me et parcas ei.

"Charles! What does it mean?"

It means, 'take me and spare him'; she wouldn't get Latin until next year.

My boots pounded the wobbly path. The cemetery gate came into sight. I grabbed the edge of the black gate and pulled myself onto the sidewalk, where I toppled against one of the trees.

I could see her standing there. She held forth my bloody writing.

Deep beneath the old graveyard, the zombie mushroom peeled the red bricks apart like a zipper, and she tripped into darkness. The zipper continued to open, inches from my feet, where the first bricks were separated by tree roots. The brick teeth snapped back into place.

It took a second before I started running, and like I said, I'm running still.

Well, here's my bus, good luck with the zombie collection.

STARDAWG

by Bertram Montiekowicz

THE PHONE RANG. I KNEW ONE DAY IT WOULD.

Again, the tin bell shivered inside its beige cage. I watched, helpless. There's only one way to make it stop.

When I offered no greeting, a woman spoke.

"I was hoping to reach Professor Mantiekowicz."

She got the pronunciation correct.

"Speaking."

Her familiar voice, like an old friend, but all I could see was gray skin, an eyeless face shackled by colorless locks.

"Professor Mantiekowicz, it's Agent Hawley."

This revelation released me:

I can see you now Agent Hawley, five eight and three quarters, larger than me, a hundred and forty three pounds of pure muscle, but her whole life was the workout, put your time in, trust results you can't see, vary the program to progress the whole.

Agent Hawley stuck to the plan, and it worked.

When the US government needed someone to torture me, she accepted responsibility with the gravity of Jupiter.

She couldn't have been too surprised when They asked her to make this call.

I affected the mock personability that annoyed everyone. "My goodness, how long has it been?"

I could hear the soft movement of her lips. "Almost ten years now."

"Wow, that long."

She said, "You kept your promise."

"I figured I'd better! Better I keep mine than you keep yours, you always—," I interrupted myself, torching the gushing wound.

I was going to say, 'you always remember your first time, especially torture.'

Closing my eyes, we were together again, me under my black hood, bent into a straight line on a thin wooden board. They treated me gentler because I was already weak, American torture is not for killing, we're trying to save lives. Drugs of course would not produce the desired effect; also, I developed certain powers over the years while living off the taxpayer's dime.

What a way for my career at MK-ULTRA to end.

"Bertran."

Ten years ago, she needed me to tell the truth, now she wanted something else.

I tracked the nervous energy in her voice, its frequency, drawn like a lonely rider to the closest tower, bounced into heaven and back to earth, her wasted heat suddenly near, coursing through my switching station, along miles of crucified wire, this road no one followed, a circuitous route, man returning copper to the mountain, knifing it through my walls, concealed by red white and blue plastic. I could tell Agent Hawley was scared.

This was supposed to be a safe house.

The phone became too hot to press near my face.

She said, "I appreciate your willingness to take my call."

"I always thought we might have been friends, I—." So many cruel things we can say to each other whenever we want.

"The reason I'm calling—."

"I was going to send you a card, afterwards, afterwards... I actually thought about it, a year after, you know, our little time together, like an anniversary. I was going to invert a Get Well Soon card, but then I thought you might not get the joke, you know, think I was making some threat or provocation, or perhaps even a prevarication." I tried to breathe, unsure if either of us actually knew what that word meant. To be clear I added, "I certainly didn't want you to visit."

There were muted persons on the line, others near Agent Hawley making gestures, mouthing commands. I should have known.

My growing smile meant the levee had overflown, threatening a torrent of the inappropriate, TOI, a term my girlfriend conceived before she ran off with my baby in her belly; let's call her Presto, because she disappeared. Presto liked TOI because it made clear what I did was worse than TMI, further along; how many times she wished upon reaching M, I could see N and O.

I opened my mouth but nothing came out. It must be true, grow or die.

Agent Hawley said, "Professor, allow me, on behalf of the US government, and my FBI in particular, what happened ten years ago was a mistake, and while you never came forward publicly, which we appreciate—that was a real pro move on your part, everybody said so—but I urge you, we urge you, accept this financial compensation the Grand Inspector General says you're entitled to... I understand you're not doing that well right now—."

"I'm doing fine! I'm doing great!"

"Professor, let's dispense with the small talk. Unfortunately, you've probably figured out, this is no mere reunion call, and this check that's sitting here with your name on it, if you don't want it, please take it instead as a fee for services. Your first government job was fee for services, wasn't it? What was that, 1962? Well, we need your help again Professor."

My smile lost some of its vitality.

Agent Hawley was all business, even when the business was making it seem like it wasn't business, even when the business was just waiting, doing nothing, or working opposite, a set up, a detour, she needed you off course, away from familiar pathways, then she could steal me into the darkness that surrounds everything I've ever known, where earth is but a speck. Once so lost, only she could tell me where I was going, only she could lead me back; I followed then, and felt more than ready to follow now, like a stray dog, hungry and homeless, I would do anything for the barest acknowledgment.

Agent Hawley ran a different game this time, revealing both faces as fake; she had a closet full of them. Her poor husband, he probably doesn't know who he's sleeping with from one night to the next. Maybe he likes it like that. They can play bad cop bad cop.

She didn't seem to know what I was thinking about. "Bertran, I have to ask you a question. Over the past twenty-four hours, have you seen a TV screen or listened to a radio, had any contact with the outside world?"

After a pause I said, "You know, this really takes me back—you would say, 'Bertran, I have to ask you a question' even though you already knew the answer, and then what would I do?"

She paused, trying to match my tempo. "You had a number of responses, as I recall; listen, Bertran, you understand, I represent the US government, it could be said I speak for the President. If you would please turn on the TV, you'll see what's happening, and why we need your help."

Searching for traps, I moved forward into the darkness. "Ok, hold on."

I rested the handset with its pig tail wire on the blue vinyl countertop dividing the rooms housing my existence, home to my possessions. I can say with some certainty nothing here has any value at the nearest pawn shop. It's fallen on me to preserve their worth, only I can set the price. Price controls, price gouging, price manipulation, cartels are earth's most natural organism, call it entropy, a syndicate came to life during those three syllables. Capitalism got it wrong, and socialism, and the libertarians, their City on the Hill sank faster than Atlantis. No one can put a price on someone else's memories, their dreams, what's an old photo filled with smiling friends to someone who sees only strangers? To be with them again, when we were at our best, Maggie, Penny Nichols, Old Cally, even the bosses, to have something like that in my hands right now would be priceless, but MK-ULTRA staff were encouraged not to take pictures, especially at work.

The gunmetal linoleum beneath my worn sole could not be avoided, one carefully cut piece extending around the dividing counter, into the kitchen and bathroom/laundry room beyond. A thin strip of molding kept the synthetic material pinned against the floor, so it wouldn't move. Tiny nails had been tapped in the thin strip of wood at regular but not precise intervals, but the cramped conditions didn't bother me—think of it this way, it would be easy to show someone around, if anyone ever visited.

The TV had a tube, and knobs, the picture wasn't great. The antenna could only pick up strong local signals, but my mind hears the broadcast as it arrives on the screen. My work experiences, the drugs, they transformed me, made me like the duck-billed platypus, whose brain evolved outside its skull as the only way to survive in a world without light.

The dissonance made TV difficult to bear. My fingertips twitched, chasing shadowy soundwaves. When I don't hear anything it means something important is happening. It's usually then I turn on the TV, to find out why my brain had gone quiet, but not today, today I was free from the incessant blabber, inconsistent opinion, intellectual dishonesty, unintelligible idiocy, jealous libel, illogical fallacy, partisan rah-rah, whataboutism, red herrings, strawmen, outright lies... until now.

My last visitor joked about the TV because of its age, picture quality, my dearth of choices; I calculated how much of their life they wasted sitting in front of it, walked them through my assumptions, how to express it as a percentage of waking hours... that was the last time I saw them. Who was it? The boss? No, it was someone else I worked with, they must have targeted my memory before they left.

It didn't matter much. Now that Agent Hawley had allowed me to remember her face, everyone looks like her, my mother, my father, watching them die, as they turned to watch me die; Agent Hawley became everyone, even that one time I went out on stage, don't stare at their faces, you know you're gonna lose it, what are you even doing this for? Now it's Agent Hawley in every seat, and she hadn't even been born.

I crossed the room, two steps on my cane, and the TV came alive. You spin the dial, that's why these kids say "turn it on," they don't even know what they're talking about. The volume would go up, there was no way to avoid it. I spun the knob backwards as fast as I could, but the sudden racket caused a spasm that bent my back.

Steadied against the stand, I prayed for quiet.

Using thumb and forefinger on the channel changer, chugging between stations and keeping my balance with the other hand, the TV made clear, something was wrong with America.

On the screen, sparkling with color, liberal channels saying a secret right-wing government conspiracy exists, while conservatives said no, don't be stupid, it's a socialist conspiracy inside the secret government. I looked instead at the ant line of letters crawling across the bottom of the screen, trying to reform them into unique words. I had to blink to avoid splashes of red blood. Stillshots of sunken people with deepset eyes filled with pain pulled me further into the screen. Within twenty-four hours the world had gone mad; meanwhile, I sat serene, tapping my foot to an old tune. In fact, I hadn't felt this great for awhile. The only source of variance between me and the rest of America seemed to be I didn't give a shit what was on TV.

The dial began to move of its own accord; there's nothing like turning on the TV to make you want to change the channel. The news reporters must be clones programmed to portray the same practiced emotions. Unable to keep a secret smile knowing ratings were sky high, their boyhood friends and extended family must be so proud, my eyes locked on Ken Doll's painted mouth as it morphed, contorting into words of sorrow and horror he obviously could not feel.

The dial stopped moving my hand. I lost track of the plotline. My eyes freed themselves. I could turn the TV off. Now you know why I disconnected in the first place: one nation, under God, divisible, a parallel universe where reality's heroes and villains change capes from one global news channel to the next; but no, it's me who's lost my mind.

By the time I made it back to the phone my smile had disappeared, like standards in journalism, ethics in politics, love of country.

"So what?" I asked.

I had become accustomed to Agent Hawley's approach. Like a tennis star, her volley would find its way over the net, land inbounds, force me to react too fast, always reaching, hoping my next return left me less vulnerable.

She asked, "What can you tell us?" She paused for emphasis and her earnestness disarmed me momentarily.

"It looks like a lifetime of sowing disinformation has finally borne fruit."

She asked, "Were you able to gather any facts?"

"On TV? Of course not."

"Ok, let me—."

"No, you need not bother. I understand completely. Only the FBI knows the real truth, but I guess that makes sense, right, you're the one snooping everybody, whether it's MLK or Trump, you're not picky. You opened the file on Malcolm X while he was still in prison—."

Then the other her joined us, the one I knew too well.

"Listen to me, Bertran. There's no time to waste. We're coming to get you right now, so please, just come along quietly."

I stood frozen, listening for what would be next, the whir of a helicopter blade in the distance, slicing the air, cutting off any chance of escape, the sound, another hack to disable me. Boots on the ground, a perfunctory knock on the door before the key turned; I was locked in.

Several faded images of myself approached, reflected in the soldiers' polished rifles. I looked shrunken and weak, like always. When they were close enough I could see the cheap phone dangling alongside my open jaw. Two unarmed soldiers stepped forward, both Captains, and wordlessly lifted me from my place. A third grabbed the cane as it fell away.

Strapped into the back of an unmarked black Chinook, helmet slapped and clapped onto my fractured skull, we lifted into the bleak dusk, assembled to it. The helicopter banked, headed back the way it came. I caught a glimpse of the desert below, staring right at me, cold. Nothing was familiar, except being taken.

Agent Hawley returned, piped through my ears. I would have yanked the helmet from my head if I could.

A new voice seemed appropriate, finally ready to expose her true self, but I knew better.

"Thank you, Bertran, for not resisting. Now, let me explain what's going on, please, I know how difficult this must be for you... I actually came to appreciate your consistency, I told everyone that, our experience with, you know, parapsychologists... let's just say, since you retired, and poor Maggie, it's been hard to find reliable partners. Are there things we can't explain? Sure, but we usually find there is some explanation. The younger generation, they think their prediction is everything, I guess we all went through that stage. This idea that change is the only thing we can count on, it's a paradox of course, but paradoxes are about as close as we get to defining reality; you taught me that. Neils Bohr, right? I'm sure you haven't forgotten."

Forgotten? No.

Remembered? Not exactly.

Torture: loud music, a parade of taxpayer financed potty-mouthed sadists, Agent Hawley knew the only thing I ever cared about was my daughter, so that was the leverage. I logged the different threats, thirty-seven in all, but the top four were replayed over and over, like Gilligan's Island, another three hour tour where no one comes back as the same person. Words I could stand, I knew how to listen. It was the lack of sleep that got me, the REM sleep where our dreams are opened. The easiest way to torture someone is to disconnect them from their dreams. I would have said anything to make it stop, praying some nightmare would whisk me away. So, no, I haven't forgotten.

For the moment it seemed she could no more read my thoughts than I could hers. Calmly she continued, not with the newsman's detachment, but the will of an executioner, whose only care is a clean cut.

She said, "We're headed to Lebanon, Kansas. The closest airport that can take the Galaxy is Salina Regional. There's another chopper waiting that will take us to Smith Center Municipal Airport. I'll be with you. We'll drive the last leg. Do you know why we're going to Lebanon?"

"Because it's the geographic center of the contiguous United States."

"That's right, Bertran, that's very good, but why are we bringing you there?"

Parapsychology had not been as enriching a career as my young self imagined. Maybe I read too much Philip K. Dick, or too little.

MK-ULTRA, what can I say. Many of us who came of age in the 60s were already busy remodeling our minds, DIY, tearing down old walls, compartments for more storage, now, why not a window that looks out on the universe?

In the 70s, after failing to change the world, my inebriated brethren turned inward, assuming if everyone fixed themselves, by virtue the world would be saved. In the 80s we just wanted the government off our back, and since the 90s brought an end to history, we celebrated. It seemed humanity's only responsibility to the new century would be to earn as much money as we could, and spend it on things we didn't need, but I felt different. I told the old boss back in the 80s, after my only promotion, cold wars end hot, it's no different than what goes up. Walls are easy to rebuild, and scared people love walls. Instead of heeding my advice They used it to help build the program.

Every step of the way I was out of step, and my erstwhile allies, the people like me, who felt like me, agreed with me, they succumbed to the test of time. My co-workers at MK-ULTRA were brilliant thinkers, despite the jokes. Like power hitters we only had to be right about thirty percent of the time to be considered Hall of Fame material. Parapsychologists, as we were generally called, like any good scientist, we learned solutions are kept in containers—whether it be a liquor bottle, pill case, drug vial, prison cell, or a cheap coffin in an unmarked grave.

The solace we searched for on the street of protest, the sense of community, lay just out of reach, behind a protective barrier. My generation loved peace so much the government had to beat it out

     STARDAWG

of us with a stick they bought with our parents' tax dollars. To fight for what's right is exhausting and came at the expense of family, hobbies, vacations. We wanted a better America and because of that, got nothing.

They said I ran away, became a hermit, gave up after the battle was over, but what are a refugee's choices? On the bus, in the office, at Halloween, these last pathetic vestiges of the village, how dare the government force me to participate in a society so different than the one promised by the Golden Age of Science Fiction?

So I fled into the wilderness, to be alone, but I wrote something once myself, after retirement, before losing my mind, or perhaps while it was happening, and some people read these made up stories... no one was more surprised than me to hear I had readers. Like Archie Bunker or Dice Clay, my fans mistook the portrayals, assuming I held some kinship with the characters in my stories, what they said about the US government, which I assured Agent Hawley, time and again, I did not.

This small group of terrorists, almost like the Manson family listening to the White Album and hearing the necessary encouragement to start a race war, my readers mistook me for some important thinker, but they couldn't have been more wrong. They were bad people. One of my stories they used as an instruction manual.

My accidental cabal spread inside the government. That's how they found out who I was, where I lived, kept sending ambassadors to meet me, following me around, talking to me, buying me drinks. They claimed they took their orders from me, but how could I be a leader when I never advocated for anything other than myself?

What I said, what I wrote, they were just words to me. I told Agent Hawley that, but she tortured me for seventeen days anyway. That's what torture is for, though, right... how else could she ever trust me? I promised not to betray my country, even after it betrayed me.

Once I convinced Agent Hawley there were no hidden members in my conspiracy, on this world or another, in the past or to come in the future, I was free to go, as long as I agreed to stop writing and live out the rest of my days in a government safe house, which was nothing new. All they did was put the lock on the outside, feed me like any other circus animal.

I knew this day would come; people like me never retire.

Agent Hawley's voice in each ear, she introduced another, even more compassionate self.

"Bertran, look, I can hear your breathing, I know when you're not feeling well, you're no young man, how old are you now? We need you, Bertran, you have to stay with me, don't go to the dark place."

Oh, the one you showed me? Surely you can block my descent, even as the Chinook turns to mercury, sucked into the black hole at the center of the galaxy.

Worried, she kept going. "Let's talk about the problem. It's a puzzle. You like puzzles, don't you, Bertran? You can solve puzzles no one else can because your brain doesn't work right. Isn't that what you told me? Let's take it from the top, you know where to start, everything was normal, as it always is, spinning and spinning but staying in place... then, guess what? We see a spaceship headed for earth and it's Sputnik 2."

Readers will say, ah Bertran, how could you have known at this point it was the space dog, Laika, who had cheated death.

Agent Hawley launched into her monologue, I could picture her mouth curling around a run-on sentence. She said, "Surprise surprise, a lot of what the Russians said about Sputnik 2 wasn't true, it was just a bunch of commie propaganda. Them red bastards, you have to give it to them. They wanted us to blast money into outerspace, and it worked. It was only a month after Sputnik 1 for Christsake. There was no way they were ready for that mission, it just coincided with some commie anniversary. That and we were freaking out over Sputnik 1. I'm sure you remember. Everybody was scared the Russians would drop a nuke out of a spaceship. Senators were pulling their hair out, they wanted Eisenhower to take his concrete and build bunkers instead of interstate highways. Them commies, they made Laika a star, 'cause you know, they weren't allowed to have pop stars. The Russian scientists made no plan to return her safely. They literally just shot her straight out into space. There was a robot feeder on board that would automatically add a special poison to her food at a set time, to spare her the pain of asphyxiation. The CIA always knew the Russians were lying about their space program. The FBI knew, apparently, since '91 at least, that whatever the British observed burning up in the atmosphere wasn't Sputnik 2. In 2002, we suggested the Russians admit their robot feeder had failed and Laika suffered a terrible death, to see if anyone was paying attention, but no one cared. At that point, what could be gained exposing the Russians? We used their fake program to justify our real program. You know how it is, Bertran, I don't need to tell you, the Cold War, well hell any war, it's all psychological, the battle for hearts and minds. Victory demands we stand for something, that we act nobly, offer opportunity, prize fairness and openness, but it's a lot easier to win the actual fighting war if you can fake the rest of it. The Russians, we both stretched the truth all the way into outerspace. We wanted to see how far we could go. It might seem particularly cruel giving this stray dog a one-way ticket, but I'm sure you'll agree, there were worse crimes no one will ever hear about. So that's all I have, Bertran. Sputnik 2 is returning to earth, apparently with some modifications. We're at a loss. We've reached the limits of science. So I ask you Professor Mantiekowicz, can you solve this problem?"

Of course, of course I could, but having ideas in your head, transforming them into words, spitting them out, this process, a tongue connected to your toes, one hundred muscles responding to neurons arcing between brain cells, nature's electronics buried in my skin but extending, wireless, into the air around me, the oxygen and nitrogen combination now ammunition, released in precision bursts through the larynx, the internal thyroarytenoid vibrating to produce sound while voicing vowels and consonants is left to the cricothyroid, the only muscles not managed by cranial nerve X, which touches our heart. Just imagine this dance of delicate membranes no one can ever see. One hundred and seventy thousand words in the English language to choose from, another fifty thousand already obsolete, such a vast array to sort, search strings sifting for the right allocation, and then you're not allowed to close your eyes while you do it, you have to look at them, dumbly waiting for some utterance, as if these processes could be accomplished instantaneously under close scrutiny. We don't appreciate how much we expect from each other. Only liars are free to speak clearly.

I said, "Yes."

She paused again, perhaps noting how far I'd come.

To my surprise, my keepers simply removed the entire seat from the helicopter and clipped it into the back of the C-5M Super Galaxy. The airplane sat perched in the night like a black dragon, purring, waking only when my party crept into its chambers. In my mind's eye the creature rested atop the treasure taxpayers had spent summoning it to earth, a cool bed of nickels. Thomas Jefferson's profile suddenly turned to face me, mocking, all two billion of them, IN GOD WE TRUST indeed.

The dragon roared as soon as my seat clicked into place. How long it tested the night I could not say. The soldiers retreated, but not before encircling me with tapestries, partially to camouflage the huge airship's matte gray surface, but mostly to relieve me of its emptiness. The cloth, I guess they were bed covers, hung from the plain ceiling, and showed a pastoral scene; I noted the disguise, which produced the opposite effect, not innocent deer in a leafy grove, but meaty prey who follow blindly, knowing the weakest might be eaten alive at any moment by a pack of wolves.

 STARDAWG

My eyes locked onto what held the tapestries aloft, a black government issue zip tie. Great to see you Twisty! To survive torture you need mental discipline. Twisty was the only companion I could count on during those lonely hours because Twisty was always there. Once me and Twisty became friends, and it was rough at first, he introduced me to the rest of the gang: Boombox, Bucket, Ballsy Balsa, Barbie Wire. Twisty made it fun to meet someone new. Another board game? If you insist.

Deep breath, they always say, deep breath.

The landing rang like a warning. Agent Hawley must have known, because her voice returned.

"I'm right outside, Bertran, we're going to get you disconnected. We've got plenty of Sprite here, and also the mushrooms, but we need you to eat them right away. The spaceship is set to land in about twenty minutes, which means if we hurry we'll get there just in time. You'll be open by then."

The Galaxy came to a complete stop. I heard the hatch open, fizz like flat soda, a beginning without expectation, a sticky poison, and then there she was, pausing between two bed sheets. Agent Hawley seemed shocked by my state of deterioration. In contrast she fought aging like everything else; her life depended on it.

She said, "You're going to be fine." She began undoing the straps as I sat placidly, a toddler who's outgrown his carseat. "Can I help you walk?"

I nodded.

I liked the idea of myself as a baby, especially one who had been cared for. They didn't have carseats in my day, us kids climbed around, rode on the bumper, sometimes we hit our heads. Don't ask me to explain this barbarism to those born into a world without lead in their gasoline. I can't say the lies of corporate executives were more prodigious in my day, we just trusted them, told as they were by the best America had to offer. The untruth that killed my parents involved whether seatbelts actually worked, while my allergies stemmed from a little white lie about mother's milk, carrying with it the wisdom of the ages, not being good enough for any precious boy.

None of the military types offered me any recognition, going by The Book. I can barely remember the helicopter ride that followed. Agent Hawley held my hand, as she used to do.

"Bertran, can you hear me?"

I looked at her, those ponderous blue eyes, stark behind thick lashes, a magic pool in a fairy forest, a familiar illusion that came to me in dreams, not as you might expect, being pulled down by a tentacled leviathan, but me floating above the water, dried out, having been wrenched from the womb with forceps by an impatient doctor, and crippled because of it. Earth had been ruined, America perverted, that's how I woke, but not in a sweat because I couldn't afford heat; if the choice is between medicine, food, and basic needs, I'll shiver every night, it was something I learned how to do as a child. Some things you can never forget.

"Bertran, I need you to eat these mushrooms, can you do that for me? I have a Sprite here as well."

"The doctor said I had to quit soda."

"That's ok, that's fine, whatever you want. Just let us know, but you've got to get these mushrooms down right now, ok?"

One thing I learned over my long career, when the FBI insists you eat a hallucinogenic mushroom, you do it.

The next minutes, which most people felt building up to something, were no different than any other moment to me. This is how I spent my life, expecting the next trip. The road stretched out, not before or behind, but alongside on both sides.

I knew almost immediately it was a terrible mistake.

There I was, in the queue at my government financed graduation, black gowned, square hatted, waiting for them to mess up my name so I could limp onto the dais, but instead of a diploma the dean handed me regret.

No one cheered.

As they helped me from the stage I realized the others, cloaked like me, had been given something else, even their faces were different. I clutched the regret, wanted to get rid of it, but no one wanted it. Someone explained I had to wait for the quiet of death. I turned back to the stage, to protest, but the Dean had become the President of the United States, one I recognized, an amalgamation of JFK's privileged opportunities, LBJ's bullying instinct, Nixon's natural duplicity, Carter's end of empire interventionism, Reagan's market worship, Bush's sinister secrecy, Clinton's lying passion, the next Bush's patriotic idiocy, Obama's false hope, Trump's unshakable narcissism, and Biden's dumb act, wrapped up in one person, every president I could remember, all exactly the same.

The helicopter must have landed some time ago, bumping along inside silent sirens, flashing lights plowed our way.

Agent Hawley waited patiently. "Are you ready to tell us how the dog could have survived so long alone, how it might have made the necessary adjustments to Sputnik 2, why it charted a course for the center of the United States?"

"Yes."

I could hear the seconds ticking like a villain's time bomb.

She lost patience. "And?"

I said, "She must be some bitch."

The soldier in the front passenger seat turned to face me, I guess in curiosity, or perhaps thinking I spoke in jest. Under the helmet I saw his peachy face would soon burn away, blackened like salmon. I was back in my parents' car. I dared not turn to where my father sat, to see again that fiendish grin. The soldier's eyes were steady, encased in the same bony crust as his face, the helmet and skull were melded together. This troglodyte, after being entombed in an underwater grave for millennia, had resurfaced for sick but unknown reasons. Then I knew why, it wanted to snuff out the light of life, jealous of what had been forever lost. That's why only killing made sense. Was it a smile, the line that split the monster's face, and grew into the leer of a Jack O'Lantern, cracking further still, like the edge of the earth at the end of time. The crack grew until the black shell fell away, revealing the ugly face of the killer lurking inside, and it was my own.

I heard Agent Hawley say "Stop the car" over my screams. She took the soldier's place in the front seat and looked back at me, to replace the image; she knew how it worked, as crazy as that must sound.

Next thing I know we're there at the landing site, it looked like the movie, Spielberg called it, the ring of equipment, focus of lights, a semi-circle of solid-colored suits and mottled uniforms. Agent Hawley waited patiently for my return, knowing from the vacant stare no answers would be forthcoming.

"You said Laika is a bad bitch, what did you mean?"

I turned to her briefly. "Dogs have an instinct for home. In 1923 Bobbie the Wonder Dog walked twenty-five hundred miles from Indiana to Oregon. He probably walked right by here." I looked for evidence. She regained my attention; her impatience was palpable but I mistook it for disbelief. To convince her, I said, "You're probably thinking, well that was a long time ago, but what about Bucky? Walked five hundred miles from Virginia to his home in Myrtle Beach, and that was in 2012. Then there was Moon, a Siberian Husky—."

"Professor, I was interested in something you said."

She used this line to train me, no different than, 'Do you want to go for a walk?' My chance to enjoy freedom at the end of a leash. What she said next, I could not say.

Events sped. Soldiers and suits changed places, a landfill, mismatched parts discarded by civilization, dumped here in the middle of nowhere, with nowhere to go and nothing to do, just stink up the place with their rot. This lasted for a long second, then everything dissolved in a slow instant, hard lines of definition gave way, colors melted into brown like crayons in a microwave, or mismatched Play-doh. I suddenly realized where we were... it was Circle V in Upper Hell, where the violent sinners rise up to renew their earthly rivalries, but they can only do so if they stand on the sullen, those who in life did nothing to prevent the violence, whose sighs can be seen bubbling up through the mud. One of these sighs exploded nearby, striking my cheek with a stony clump of dirt, but when I reached up, it was just the familiar piece of broken beer bottle embedded in my face since my father's vehicular murder suicide.

Agent Hawley knew from the spastic movement things were not going well. She seized the back of my elbow, another lever she left in place, rusty maybe, but it still worked. She asked, "How could this have happened?"

"Divine intervention, Aliens, Gods, what's the difference? A higher power. If The Bible is right, and God made man in his image, then God must be a dog lover. Feels like payback."

Sputnik 2 descended, neon green luminescence, fire, water, wind and now, earth.

She asked, "What can we do?"

"I suggest you listen."

She lost the thread for a moment, a becoming innocent look, forgotten keys, fallibility. I had been trained to assist and could not bear to watch. "To the dog."

She refocused. "The dog will speak to us."

"Of course, what do you think, she wants to run and jump into Korolev's arms? If that was true she'd be headed for Lake Vivi."

"No jokes now, this is the same dog that left earth in 1957?"

"Yes."

"Returning with a message."

"Yes."

"Feels like payback."

"Definitely."

She seemed satisfied enough to take a pause and shared a look with some gray haired General who had been listening since my phone first rang. We turned to each other. I could sense he suspected I was involved, that my thirteen-year-old self had some role in today's events, that I was a little commie symp, a pinko, a red. A lifetime in uniform convinced him no one could ever love America as much as him. MK-ULTRA agents were looking into the past and future all the time. For the military men, our role in the campaign was unreliable, untrustworthy, what good are wizards to a paladin. Whenever things went south some bloated military aristocrat would call us in, dare to ask why none of us saw it coming. Needless to say, the cooperation between our particular brand of CIA asset and the old-school military types was never a close one.

As the cone-shaped capsule settled carefully on the rocky outcropping, displaying a novel rocketry, we were each left to marvel. Somehow I knew the craft employed a hydrogen drive, as that would make the most sense, using for fuel what the universe held in abundance, the simplest element.

Snipers, machine guns, cannons, every piece sat on the board. I sensed these weapons would soon fire, and the smell from this vision, sulfur and phosphorus, made its way along the tendrils of my inner nose membrane, slipping unseen between my eyes, hardened into wire; I felt the wire puncture my optic nerve, where it began sending images to my brain. My nose ran, a headache followed. The invisible wire must have been forged with the iron in my blood as strengthless, the cane slipped away. Before cracking my head Agent Hawley went to one knee and gently caught me, as if we'd practiced for a live audience.

Then the spaceship door opened and Laika stepped forward onto the makeshift landing platform, where she stood, proud but serious, like the rest of us from the 50s, grayed by time. Laika had been rescued from the streets of Moscow and was of unknown breed. I noticed she did not meet our stare. The dog's eyes held the sadness anyone might show after being betrayed, abandoned, used, left alone to starve and die in the coldness of space, but could she have known we learned next to nothing from her sacrifice?

As I lay in Agent Hawley's arms, I felt so lost. I couldn't help but wonder, is this story about me, or her? And if my soul, my only form of existence, has been reduced to this scramble of alphanumeric symbols, some fiction, where is the other character, the one who rips us apart or binds us together forever, the performer whose appearance on stage reveals whether we're watching a comedy or a tragedy, as we only get to choose between the two.

Then I heard his voice, the Commander in Chief. "What the hell is going on over there?"

I guess he was here in this hell with us the whole time. The man himself could not be seen or smelled, a most welcome disembodiment. Each member of our well respected, well trained and well equipped military was forced to follow his every command by an old piece of paper. The president's voice carried a panic that went far beyond any zombified dog, and he was eager to share his feelings with us. In the president's tone and words I could hear dissatisfaction and disappointment, but also what it must be like having everyone kiss your ass, for years and years. To the president, when someone tried to kiss his ass, it revealed good judgment; anyone else can never be trusted. People flattered him to get what they wanted, and he believed them.

The president concluded his remarks unabated by my dismissive thoughts. "What are you idiots doing?"

The General was quick to respond. "Sir?"

"You're broadcasting!"

"Sir, there's no broadcast."

"Dogs are going crazy, we've all been bit."

I could tell the president was lying and had not been bit.

The General said, "Sir—."

Then I heard it, I guess everyone did, military dogs, another weapon in the arsenal. They were in a suitable vehicle parked over the ridge, and were tearing it apart, bursting out with broken glass. Shouts and a scuffle ensued. Silence won with three quick shots. A wave of sadness rippled across the landscape: soldiers had killed the dogs they loved.

Nothing could stop the president from yelling. "We can see it's coming from your location!"

The fool had once again confounded the numbskulls; Agent Hawley knew when to be quiet, and this moment, lying together, the president on the line, I suddenly felt the urge to speak. Despite my long career, and because of it, I could never get this close to any president. Few do. Imagine somebody is working for you but you can only tell them they're doing a shitty job every four years. I thought, if I dare speak, it should be big, memorable. If you could tell this president one thing, what would it be?

"Mr. president, sir, please, sir, would you shut the fuck up."

"Who said that? Who said that?" He wouldn't even let me finish. I pictured his disfigured face, fake hair and spray paint skin, dusty fat folds well tailored, a made for TV monster.

The operations line opened, one of the field units, "Sir, we have movement atop the dog, say again, movement on the dog's collar, ducking now behind the fur."

"Get it up on the screen!"

"I want to know who said that!"

The military men seemed happy to ignore their Commander in Chief. The glee with which they proceeded showed how much they wished this moment could last forever.

We faced the screen.

Now they knew what it was like to be me, to see reality for what it is, warped. We were looking at God, or an Alien, who had found our lost puppy, and brought her back to life, used her instinct to set a course for earth. The Being couldn't have been more than two inches tall, but its miniscule mouth worked furiously.

The General yelled, "Give me audio!"

You think the president could stop yelling at this moment?

"If you don't tell me who said that I'm going to court martial every last one of you! General! General! Goddammit!"

But their discipline demanded my identity remain hidden; I wasn't even supposed to be here. The president has to live in the same need-to-know world as the rest of us. They never seem to get it. That's when we Watergate them.

The technicians tinkered with the sound until we could hear the same frequency as a dog. It was the tiny alien barking.

The president quickly reacted, like in the movies. "That's the signal you idiots, cut it off!"

I guess the team in the war room under the White House had already figured it out, but instead of using normal channels the president had unnecessarily inserted himself, wanting to be in the middle of the operation for political reasons, to take a fake picture like when Obama's team acted like they were killing bin Laden. You never seen a body though, did you? Trust your government.

The soldiers and suits looked around in confusion. Out of my view, some man of action said, "The Alien must be using the President's non-secure line to broadcast nationally."

The General pushed a button, cutting off his commander in mid scream. The president's removal from the scene lifted a burden from everyone in earshot, a spell broken, cobalt clouds rent asunder by gold sunlight.

One of the team members said, "We're still broadcasting."

The General said, "We're going to have to destroy the equipment."

Another asked, "What about the vehicles?"

Agent Hawley's rubbery skin cushioned us against the press of my weak frame on her body armor. We looked at each other as equals, and I understood what the Alien was doing.

I said, "It's using our bodies to send the signal. It's not the equipment you need to destroy, but each other." I looked the old soldier in the eye. "Kill us all, General, while you still have a chance."

Agent Hawley also turned, and we both sensed the General's disappointment. At war school they taught him how to count bodies, to weigh the sacrifice of those he orders to die, but these calculations become more variable once you're part of the equation.

The operations line remained open. "We have a shot General."

"Well take it Goddammit!"

The sniper's finger barely twitched. I watched the bullet make its way, only to ricochet off some invisible shield the Alien maintained. This opening of hostilities, and its lack of success, spurred others to squeeze, and I did the same, with my eyelids. The sound would soon kill me. I swung my left arm, crashing into the General who held his place nearby. "Tell them to stop shooting!"

Agent Hawley understood my life was at stake. She grabbed me, made me look into her eyes, said the magic word, unchained me.

I rolled out of her arms, onto all fours. My ears didn't hurt any more.

The barrage ended. As the smoke dissipated we could see the Alien's shield held. Fifteen trillion budgeted for national defense since The Wall came down and still no weapon against God. In the moment of realization and resignation that followed, Laika and I shared a look, perhaps because I was the only person on all fours.

I understood what I needed to do. I locked Laika's eyes, filled my lungs and let out one long howl. I couldn't speak Laika's language, but I could tell her how I felt. I could say sorry, sorry for what the human race did to dogs, the way we bred you to our needs, taking loyalty for granted while mistaking friendship for subservience.

I tried to reach back a hundred thousand years and feel the pain the first man felt when he lost his dog, and the first dog who lost her man, and everyone in between. I tried to meet the dog halfway, to show her half the love, half the dedication, half the utility she had given humankind.

And Laika heard me, head turned slightly, one ear cocked.

Agent Hawley shouted, "It's working!"

The General dropped to the ground and picked up the sorrowful howl; any tactic that could save his own skin seemed plausible. The others followed his lead, a sound rose up. Even Agent Hawley offered a groan, but she remained sitting on the ground.

This gesture from humanity, it touched Laika, and she forgave us. Her eyes showed sorrow, no longer for what she endured, but because she had become the cause of more suffering, shepherding an Alien whose angry barks incited dogs of every breed, sending them wild, turning them against masters posing as friends. Laika loved people. She boarded a spaceship with no chance home simply because we asked her to.

We've all seen dogs teased with a treat, who with a jerk of the head bring the biscuit into their maw. That's what happened. She shook and the Alien fell, but before hitting the ground Laika swallowed the Being in one gulping bite. The broadcast ended, and with it, the

Dog Revolt. Whatever Alien power kept Laika alive drained away, and she dissolved into debris that drifted off the wind. The special adaptations to Sputnik 2 self-destructed and many were killed, including Agent Hawley, separated into two pieces by a twirling sheet of aluminum moving at twice the speed of sound.

In the aftermath, the story shifted to the General's claim he saw me flick one finger, that the panel moved unnaturally in response, basically that I used telekinesis to murder Agent Hawley in a revenge killing, but my lawyer made the General look like an idiot on the stand. After another grueling trial I was acquitted by the Secret Grand Jury, avoiding the death penalty again, although the court agreed I remain a national security risk, and sentenced me to Special Remand for the balance of my days.

THE RED LAKE

by Paradox Pollack

"I NEVER KNEW IT BEFORE, BUT YOU'RE ALL REFLECTIONS. ALL OF YOU."

That's a memory—an old film quote. I love films, especially the old black-and-white ones. I'm watching someone in a reflection. A shop window pane of dark glass in the night, a single street lamp creating a spotlight for this guy. I've been here a long time watching him work. It's been a good night at the cinema. He's been convulsing for hours, always moving. I've changed my perspective, getting over his shoulder to watch his reactions, shifting to medium to check his attention and wide shots to see how the world saw him.

It's deep into the night. Hours ago, there were people all around moving from one location to another, fulfilling their own transient lives. Now it's just me and him.

"Midnight is a lonely time to be staring at strangers." A staccato string section is making it a dramatic scene from a Hitchcock film. The world is suspended until the horns begin to swell, and then something shifts. Everything comes clear, and when I look back, he's different. There are two of him. One out of sync and at a strange angle.

After a few seconds, I get the focus right. The flutes rise, delicate and trembling, and then I see him. Recognition catches like the spread of black on burning paper. The heat starts in my heart, a secret ember hidden under ash. I've been suppressing it all day. I didn't want to see it. I didn't want to know. But it's me. The man in the glass—it's me.

And then, as if the reflection itself rewinds time, I see another version of me. Fresh-faced, confident, tilting my head just so, checking my reflection on the way to work. My younger self, preening in this very window. My daily ritual: a brief pause to admire my charm, my posture, the cut of my jacket. A small, narcissistic indulgence before stepping into the world. I stagger and catch myself as the memory slams into me. I've been standing here all day, circling this spot, laughing at the man in the glass, amazed at how broken he looked, how lost. I was trying to figure out how to capture it, a photo in a scrapbook.

I lean closer to the glass, searching for details, but they refuse to come into focus. The image is blurred, sagging, ragged at the edges. Now, all I see is a distorted outline, a smudge of who I was, and I can't stop looking as if I could pull the focus back into place and find who I was and who this is. The man in the glass stared back, his eyes ringed with shadow, the glass rippling as if it were a lake reflecting firelight. A vestigial ghost of innocence in the way of my slowly growing pain.

Even closer to my reflection and the glass, taking it to an extreme close-up. I'm looking for a reaction. There is no steam from my breath on the glass. I search for the dilation of the retina, but what I see is an abyss gazing back. I know that quote, and I'm finding it's true—gazing right back.

The angle of my body is different from how my body feels. I seem to have come loose from time. I gaze at the skewed angles of him and me. My eyes are asphyxiated, gasping for air. Under the darkness is a growing burning. It is so familiar. I haven't felt it all day.

I can't both be wrong. I lean in, trying to align the two. That's when I see it. My eye dangling just out of its socket, dragging the world with it.

The eye? I'm not shy about the eye. This isn't the first time this has happened. Torn fingertips on the tender, slick skin of the orb and see the shape of my fingers. Torn skin, red and cracked, streaked with soot and city grime. I have to work to not pierce my own delicate sight with the spread ridges at the black edges of crusted wounds. I get the right angle after a dozen tries and push it past a liminal socket until I hear a submerged pop. Suddenly, I saw that only one of me was staring back. The one that I have learned to hate.

Life's tough, ain't it? Perception was once owned by the person who was born with it. Now, it's more of a collective sport we are all forced to play. It's not possible to own anything unless you were born to it. Yeah, life sucks now for 99% of us. Pan across the millions of faces that blur to billions of faces and try to imagine getting to know more than a dozen. People love their demagogues and superstars more than their wives and children.

See, that's it. People don't believe in heroes anymore. That's been the real problem for a long time, but it keeps getting worse. We traded them for explosions and special effects. I used to love old Hollywood because it gave us something to aspire to. Now? It's all recycled techniques, nihilism wrapped in computer graphics and tentpole sequels. A plastic bag and plastic cup seem to agree with me as they spill out of the rusted green-painted dumpster and get whipped in the wind. The hollow echo of their crinkle and tok-tok-tok seem to fill the wide expanse of the Walnut Street alley.

"You know what's wrong with the world? People don't believe in heroes anymore." That's a classic cinema quote. I am trying to remember the film, but I'm sure it was in the 1940s. That's my mind, like a sieve. That film was written in 1946, and it's still true. Now I remember, it's "Sergeant York." It's a cliche, but I'm facing this personal crisis and was hoping to do it alone. Unfortunately, you are here, and I'm with you, so let's take the slow train to hell and burn together.

Dissolve to the flashback montage where I recall the dozen times each day that I've tried to kill myself: A blade hesitates. A noose slips loose. A cliff edge beckons, then blurs. Each time, something stops me, something that wants me to keep moving. In each sequence, there is a sunlight that shines or a warm feeling that I turn to. I'm not numb. It's not for lack of feeling. There is definitely a big "I" who is screaming constantly, but that person isn't me anymore; it's some desperate part of me clawing for death. I realize that while I've been thinking, I've been slamming against the wall next to the glass for a while. At least it stops the burning. It's a kind of compulsive disease where there is no control.

I've been haunted for weeks—a lake of shimmering red rippling under a rain of fire. I don't know if it's memory or madness, but it lingers at the edge of every waking moment. I'm talking about it because the burning keeps growing. I've been here too long. I have to move. After a few seconds, I stop myself before smashing the glass and looking around.

Empty street. Lucky me. Let's see what happens next.

I'm not dead yet. I've done everything I can to numb myself, but now what I feel is heat under thin, cracking ice that itches. The itching won't go away. I spend most of the day trying not to scratch and then the rest of the night running—just running. It doesn't matter how much of me wants to just lay down and rot—I run.

I can't put my finger on it (maybe because I have so few of them left), but when I stop moving, the itching turns to burning. I'm not just burning on the surface of the skin; I'm swimming in red water, broiling basted in a kind of saturating oil that makes every cell scream.

The more stillness, the deeper the burn and the more impossible the itch. The earth put a volcano in me.

I'm about ready to erupt. A sore full of puss that has reached the limit of the skin, just waiting to be released. If I'm still for even a moment, the fire will start to eat me. So I move on. Atrophied and stiff in my knee, I tilt and hobble with my itching feet, playing a Mozart piano sonata of wriggling worms. Out into the night. The burning rages while the itching tumbles me forward in my shambling staccato dance. I move to forget. To forget the itching. To forget the fire. To forget how I ended up like this. Yet, as I run, I drift out of my current hell and trance into memories about how I got here.

I could have done lots of things, but I was bored most of the time. No subjects kept my mind for more than a few minutes. I was raised on the web. I remember my early years just scrolling and scrolling, an endless waterfall of color and sound punctuated by memes and punchlines. If I tried to focus for more than a few minutes, this daemon was on me. The need for more. More is a strange thing to need because it isn't anything specific. It's just what is at the bottom of the screen, on the next page, around the next corner.

I never had a career. Friends called me Modem because they said I was "dialing it in." Someone said it once at a party when most of my friends were high on acid in my buddy's flop house on Spring Garden Street. I can't remember any of their names now - my mind is always on fire. I remember this: It was on Spring Garden Street, They said it, They laughed, it sucked, The name stuck. I guess not having a memory has one perk; I no longer muddy my mind with people who don't respect me.

Back then, I didn't care about careers or ambition. Anywhere the wind blew, you know. Maybe I had been betrayed too many times. Perhaps it was the wrong kind of love my parents gave me; maybe I was just too bored to ever outgrow my own laziness. Whatever it was, I drifted. So when I saw an ad for an experimental drug trial, I signed up without a second thought. Free food, a comfy bed, and old movies to pass the time? It sounded perfect.

The trial was supposed to treat obsessive behavior. Funny, right? The guy who couldn't focus on anything trying to cure his obsession with nothing. I signed more forms than I'd ever seen before, but it felt like coming home. The sterile smell of bleach and pine (it burned the back of my throat), the hum of fluorescent lights (sometimes flickering as the Drexel hospital where we did the experiments was built in the 1800s). There was something soothing about it—being told where to be, what to eat, when to sleep. No choices, no pressure. Just routines and rules I didn't have to make for myself. It was like outsourcing my existence.

The first two days were blissfully uneventful. I ate, slept, watched my classic noir (I could order whatever films I wanted), and joked with the staff. But something was off. The food tasted faintly metallic, and my dreams grew sharper. I could feel the edges of them punching through like a hole puncher through paper. By the second night, I woke up sweating through my sheets, the sterile air suddenly too thick to breathe.

Two days in, the burning started.

First, my torso was warm, and then my head began to swing like a broken pendulum, back and forth, an unsteady rhythm I couldn't stop. I had a dream where I saw a silver-tinted light where I could see all of the bacteria and small living creatures. I could sense microbes making their way across the bedsheets and in the dark corners of the room. When I woke up, it didn't stop. It was the same. My sheets were stained with sweat, and I could see the salt crystals shimmering in the threads and the bacteria curling and contracting.

I tried to report it, but it was three in the morning, and only security was awake. Fred and I were talking, and I knew I sounded pretty crazy. It occurred to me that the kind of job he had wasn't paying him enough to listen to a crazy, so I was about to turn around and watch "Don't Bother to Knock." It was on the list of films and the only black and white. I thought at first that the curators of the cinema for the Drexel University pharmacology studies must have been run by a creep when I saw something glowing around the security guard's head.

Jump cut. Flash forward.

Funny how I ended up here, isn't it? Nestled among the decaying charm of an abandoned house in the heart of Passyunk Square, a silent sanctuary shared with my rat companions. It's humble and filled with the rustling chatter of my tiny, whiskered flatmates. They offer me sustenance, simple and guiltless, and have become my squeaking comrades in this solitary existence.

I'm listening to them fight again. They fight every night. Sometimes, he is wild and destructive. Sometimes, she just picks fights, but the way he makes her suffer for her baiting and the way they make up and score their drugs and then moan for an hour or so until they use and disappear into each other's depths. Feeling them so close makes the itching harder for me to bear. I'm ashamed to say what part of my body I lost first. I don't care anymore, but there is something that keeps the burning and itching going. It feels like a life, a soul, a willingness to struggle through the feelings, but every few nights, after waiting and staring and listening to the night be released into the howling of the city and its raging machine, I can sometimes sleep. The dream has been the same for the last few nights.

I just got home from my run. I ran almost 20 miles to Souderton, hoping that my feet would break, but the itching filled them, and if I ran faster, the bones seemed to scream, and the screaming made them stronger. I think I could run for a thousand years.

Most of them are dead already; they just aren't aware, walking around in a haze of in-between. It seems obvious to me, but what do I know? I've been wandering here for what seems like a century, but it is probably only a few years. I look for the constants. There are too many random details out there in the world, and I get distracted, but I found my gravities and constants. Constants like the neighbors. The squat house junkie lovers I listen to nightly. I have other senses that have honed over the time that I wander between life and death. I wander between life and death. That's what makes me different. I think it is the thing that makes me unique. I don't hover like a cancer patient lying in a puddle of my own pain and regrets. I have the legs to do something about it. I am never sure how long I will have before I am called out for what I am and sliced, vivisected for their experiments in some lab under a thousand microscopes to understand how I got to be in this state. Still, the truth is that I got here because I was lazy. I was lazy and something having to do with my luck, which I am one billion percent convinced is terrible, but sometimes I wonder.

When I look at how much people fight or are willing to put up with complicity in a war world, it seems certain that I have some benefit over all of those suckers.

The symphony of your quarrels became the soundtrack to my evenings, punctuating the eerie stillness of the night. Your words were a striking flint, igniting a storm of accusations and recriminations. Each conflict echoes the last, and each resolution is more transient than its predecessor. Your cycle of dysfunction—your fights, your make-ups, your quests for the next fix, your cries of carnal release— each act of your tragic play fed the inferno within me, made my insides sear, and my outsides stretch and tear.

As I lurked in the shadows each night, I was unwittingly drawn into the theater of their conflict. She was as cruel as a hairpin, sharp and unyielding. At the same time, he possessed the endurance of a prizefighter, weathering each verbal blow with almost admirable resilience. Their bouts of conflict, both verbal and physical, morphed into a grotesque form of entertainment for me. A diversion from my torment, their long hours of fighting became a window into a world I no longer belonged to. Over time, fragments of their past trickled

THE RED LAKE

into their heated exchanges, painting a picture of lives steeped in privilege and dysfunction. I began calling them Katherine and Cary. Katherine hailed from generations of lowbrow aristocrats, a lineage rife with intrigue and a deeply ingrained sense of entitlement. Her tales, often laced with venom, depicted her family as a pack of greedy rodents, hoarding their wealth like perpetual winter was on the horizon. The source of their fortune was shrouded in mystery, but her disdain for them was as apparent as the moonlit night.

On the other hand, he was the progeny of fame, the son of an athlete whose name seemed to carry weight in the world of sports. Rumors hinted at a boxer of significant renown. He had sustained an injury somewhere in his career, got hooked on Oxycodone, and ended up as a low-level dealer and high-level user. Still, my disconnection from the living world and the limitations of my current existence meant I could not delve deeper into his story. My days casually browsing the Internet in libraries were long behind me; my smell alone necessitated outdoor spaces or, at the furthest edge, tall ceiling malls, another casualty of my transformation. Still, my disconnection from the living world and the limitations of my current existence meant I could not delve deeper into his story.

This pair and the TV Veteran formed the fragile threads that connected me to the remnants of my humanity. Their lives, so starkly different from mine, were a reminder of the diversity and complexity of human existence. In their bickering, in their moments of vulnerability and fleeting tenderness, I found a reflection of the life I once knew. Their struggles, though vastly different from mine, reminded me of the universal nature of human suffering and the inexorable pull of our baser instincts.

As I observed them night after night, I couldn't help but wonder about the paths that led them to this point, about the choices and circumstances that shaped their destinies. In their story, I saw the echoes of every story, a tapestry of human experience that was now forever beyond my reach. This is the reason I listen to them battle nightly.

My one and only serious partner, Jackie, told me that I was a disaster and would never amount to anything. She was cruel and focused, precise, and brilliant. The woman reminds me of her. She is brilliant, like a viper; she manipulates and then stalks him and then attacks and poisons just enough to keep him alive, and he is brilliant and plays his little keyboard like a genius. They are fighting again. I remember what that was like. Cradling my opinions like they mattered. Needing to be precise and trying to win at all costs. I can hear her through the walls, "It's not like I haven't forgiven you a hundred times for how you fucked up," and he replies, "I stopped attacking you for your flirting." "Whenever I'm not at home, I know you watch porn." Denials and pleading, and each finds a righteous way to make their point and push the other one to bow to their will. Then, they push each other when words no longer work. There is violence that I feel in the skin I have left as if it were my own. Then, after a time, they get silent. I know that they are kissing (which makes my mouth swell; lips, tongue and gums expand making my teeth feel like knives).

It seems that no matter how much they get to a place of calm and peace after lovemaking and laughing and managing the bills, there is always some tiny thing that sends her into a spasm of rage. I listen through the wall. I've been here for a few months. I was drawn through the night and heard them. It's how I found this little corner inside the walls where I live. My pack of stolen goods for cleaning my costumes so that I can walk in the everyday world, a few candles and matches, and a mattress that I found and dragged here.

They made their way out to the edge like me. The only other person on the block is a veteran of Desert Storm who was probably too old to fight back in the 80s but somehow got in and fought. Watching him is like glimpsing another world, one where innocence might

THE RED LAKE

still exist. He clings to it as if the past could rewrite the present, and somehow, he has gotten to watch all of the shows that he loved as a child. Captain Kangaroo, Sesame Street, Mr. Rogers neighborhood. He just watches them on YouTube constantly on a second hand computer he saved for. He is bald and damaged somehow from wounds in the war. I heard him speaking to his daughter, who lives far away one night. His tears afterward sunk deep into my own.

I watched Mr. Rogers as a kid, but I always felt like somehow, if I watched him, I was cheating myself. He was too kind, too friendly, maybe too honest. I felt that his neighborhood was unreliable because the world just wasn't made like that. But now, from my inside-out rare air puzzle-minded perspective, trying to walk myself back between the living and the dead, I hear Fred differently.

I hear his pleas as a last attempt for God to appear on the earth as a compassionate man wanting children to feel their feelings and accept themselves because he knew that that was the only way for the war to end. The small wars, the subtle wars. Not only the wars that get young men killed, crippled or empty but the subtle wars that make people wander as the living dead. I've learned to love my neighbors in a sticky, hungry, disgusting way. I survive in part through them. They survive in their own ways. The junkies fight and claw, their love as toxic as the needles they share. The veteran retreats, building a fortress out of nostalgia. I run. My survival is a violent sprint fueled by the burning that never lets me stop. My lips crack, bleed, and scab as I smile for the first time in days thinking of that great line from It's a Wonderful Life, "Remember, no man is a failure who has friends."

Yes, shame has long since abandoned me, as have parts of my body, their absence a testament to the grotesque metamorphosis I've been subjected to. My life, if you can call it that, is now a constant struggle against a primal urge I can barely comprehend. But there remains a spark within me, a persistent smoking ember of my old self that burns me into being. It forces me to run each night, away from the urge to kill humans, until I reach the far end of the city. I yearn for the relief of sleep, for the respite of dreams, yet each night, they elude me until I run to the far end of the city and eat brains big enough to satisfy me. Philly finally exhales its nocturnal sigh, and the world itself grows quiet. The gentle consciousness of the cows I ate calms me, and sleep grudgingly takes me.

I actually get to dream. After my long run and the feeding, I can return home and dream. The burn shifts as I run, spreading from my chest to my legs, each stride defying the flames clawing at my insides, hollowing out my organs but connecting me to a different gravity, like falling horizontally. The fire doesn't stop; it spreads like smoke in the air and catches the world on fire as I move.

I've pounded the pavement all the way to Souderton again, more than thirty miles under the shadowy veil of night. I can hear the calls of the living brains of the cows out there. The split skulls they promise become a symphony of strength. Their life touches the marrow in my bones, howling with an intensity that reinforces my resolve.

With every step, I'm convinced I could outrun time itself, cutting through the veil of the ordinary definitions of space. Become immortal and never stop running. I am sure as I do this every night that if I took a human life, these new revelations would make me more than this. A crusty chrysalis behind me as I take flight and leave these piston legs for updraft wings. I was once a man, after all, and some stubborn part of me clings to that, refusing to surrender entirely to the beast I've become. And so, I run, my feet pounding the rhythm of my resistance against becoming a murderer of what I once was. It is as if the memory I have of the small boy Modem that couldn't put two thoughts together protects me from the monster I could become. He places this bonfire in me and makes me run until I find something like him, calm, gentle, unassuming. The brains of animals calm me until I can finally stop coiling in agony and slow myself to stillness.

     THE RED LAKE

I have a persistent dream. I wrote it down. I wonder if anyone will ever read it. I wrote some other things, too. My handwriting is shaky because my nerve endings are always on fire, or twitching and trembling but I'll tell you about what else I wrote.

I often consider what it is to be what I was. Though I was an outsider, a loser, a nobody, I still knew I was connected. Now, I am not. Life is like being a leaf, clinging to a branch, knowing your stem will dry and break. People can see the other leaves; they can see that they are connected to the big tree. Each person knows that their stem is drying up, and they can see that every other person has their own connection to their branch, their connection to the same source of life. That they are dying is the thing they don't want to look at, knowing they will be in a pile by the roots returning to the source returning to the soil.

I'm not made like that anymore. I don't know how I know that but I know because my blood has changed. My blood isn't like the blood of the people that I look at. I walk the streets to find the malls. I've covered myself in my Mickey Mouse hoodie. No one would ever know the difference. I make sure it's clean every day. I make sure it's perfect; immaculate. I cover my face with a hijab around my head. The ways that you can find cover are amazing. Be completely alien in plain sight. And I don't mind. I don't mind seeing how they're all the same, with the same desires. The same design with the same pantheon of hungers. My hungers are different now. I listen to a distinct voice and listen to a voice that connects them all. I see it now—threading through the air like rhizomes beneath the soil. Invisible, tangled, feeding everything. It binds them, drives them, and keeps them alive. I see it in their eyes, feel it thrumming through the air: a shared hum of wants and dreams, an unseen network feeding them, desire binds them. I can see it, even if I'm not part of it. I'm cut from it, severed. They want to be a part of it. An endless scrolling of needs and wants. My hunger listens to a different soundtrack. I have one need; to stop the burning, to stop the itching and prevent the pain. Yet my scrolling is into these fires, these desires and dreams that seem so much more alive inside, but they make my body perpetually rot without dying. I am no longer a part of them; I am separate. I feel like I'm the first of my kind—a severed leaf, floating, lost. Maybe others are wandering like me. The living dead, disconnected, no longer human but not entirely something else. Something that makes us only suck at the tips, refuse the womb, somehow an empty cocoon of humanity that is mine.

I remember a voice from "The Grapes of Wrath" whispering about shared souls: **"A fella ain't got a soul of his own, just a little piece of a great big soul that belongs to everybody."** It's old-fashioned, black-and-white morality, but it holds my murderous hunger at bay. It reminds me we're all connected somehow. I can't be with people too long; the longing gets too strong, and I can start to see their brains through their skulls. No longer just the web network of their unconscious thoughts and desires but the sound of the throbbing of the blood in their juicy pulsing skulls like a techno trance beat with my ear on the speaker. Then, I have less and less of a mind as that particular hunger grows. The less I think, the more it burns. It burns in the space between the itch and the blood, between the scab and the wound. Wound. Bleed. Scab. Crack. Scab. Itch. Wound. Bleed. The cycle never ends.

Jackie's words haunt me. I can't forget them, and I can't forgive myself for the truth in them. They ache in the corners of my body, making me fold into pain. I barely breathe anymore. When I notice, I force in air, raspy and shallow, and my expanding ribs cut my skin from the inside. I wonder if any of my organs still work.

Jackie once said, *"Mo, I can't feel your pain, but it hurts me to see you in it. And I can't fix that. I know somehow that you choose it and that hurts even more."* She left because I couldn't face my pain, and now I'm nothing but pain. Is that karma?

I see Katherine and Cary, fighting. They press their pain into each other, desperate to make the other feel what they feel—like pressing

         THE RED LAKE

sawdust into rotting walls, trying to hold something together that's already crumbling. I understand. My pain isolates me too. It stings, searing along my porous crusty skin and deep within—all at once, all the time—and some part of me wants to take it out on someone else. But I save it for the rats, the soft-eyed cows, the things that feed my hunger.

The veteran sits in his own pain, isolated, numbed by pills. We're all alone in it, trapped by what we can't share. Sometimes I fantasize about telling them my story, looking for the villains that made me this way. As if I could break the line of isolation, become something stronger together. But I know Jackie was right: it wasn't the drug company or the experiment that made me this way. It wasn't the pain or the isolation. It was me. I made the choices that hurt her and drove her away. That's the pain I can never face—and the one I can never escape.

I've become a seer of brains, an unwilling observer of their inner symphony. I can't help it. I see their sparks and feel their synaptic dances even through the walls. Each neural exchange sends shivers down my spine, a bore worm that burrows deeper with every flicker of thought. Your minds are loud, too loud—but then you sleep. And in your slumber, the noise fades to a dull hum. The nights are my purgatory. When the city finally exhales its nocturnal sigh, I escape, following the whispers of animal minds. They guide me to the hidden banquets of dumpsters in South Philly—La Mula Terca, Hardena, Stina Pizzeria, Le Virtu, and Fond. The leftovers of your feasts become my sustenance, a grotesque communion that holds the burning at bay for a time. But there are nights when the city's neon hum pulls me in another direction. I can't resist the call of Souderton, the slaughterhouses and meat plants. There, the offerings are abundant, the blood fresher. The cows' minds are quieter and softer. They calm the flames in a way your chaotic brains never could.

"There's nothing tragic about being 50. Not unless you're trying to be 25." Norma Desmond's bitter truth from Sunset Boulevard settles into my thoughts as I gorge on the scraps of Souderton's industry. Maybe there's nothing tragic about being what I've become—unless I'm trying to be human. And isn't that what I'm doing? Isn't that why I'm still here, listening to your battles and lullabies, clinging to the fringes of your world? Every night, I tell myself the same thing: tomorrow, I'll decide. Tomorrow, I'll go to the junkies or the vet. I'll reveal myself, see if they'll help me. Maybe they'll see something worth saving, some sliver of humanity left in me. Or perhaps I'll devour them.

"I killed him for money—and for a woman. I didn't get the money, and I didn't get the woman. Pretty, isn't it?"

The line from Double Indemnity echoes, cold and cruel, reminding me that failure is the only guarantee. If I reach out, I risk rejection or worse—I risk losing control. My hunger won't stop. The itching and burning won't stop. I'm running out of ways to hold myself together, running out of excuses to keep living like this. If I step into your world, what will I become? A savior clinging to the fragile threads of kindness? Or is a monster finally free to feast?

"It's a hard world for little things."

Perhaps kindness is too fragile for a world like this, and I am no exception. Tomorrow. Tomorrow, I'll decide.

A memory came to me today. I thought I had just gotten dizzy that night at the Drexel experimental lab. I thought I had just blacked out after talking with the security guard and his halo and wandered into the street. Still, last night, instead of dreaming, I lay in a liminal state and remembered.

As I watched him, I saw two things at once. Here I was in that sterile hospital, and I could also see a lake. A red lake. Fred, the security guard, was suspended over the lake. He was talking to me about films like we had each night, he was very lonely and these nights he did security may have been his only social life. Fred would complain about his wife, and I was afraid Fred was coming on to me, but then I stopped worrying about that. If he did, I would ruin him too. That's what Jackie said. She said no matter who I would be with, I would destroy them the way I ruined her. So I just enjoyed the attention and talked about old movies. Cinema classics. The kind that don't get made anymore. The kind that had writers on salary in studio apartments. Real Studio apartments, like United Artists, MGM, and Universal Pictures.

I went there once. I saw the places where they put the writers, dancers, actors, set builders, and gaffers. They all had these cute little bungalows like college dorms but separated so they could each spin out in their own ways and show up on time to set. I dreamed about those times. Obsessed over them and would go to the library to read every detail. I was happy to have someone to share the stories with.

So he was suspended over this lake of blood, and I was looking at him at the same time, and he just came undone. Black and white and then the red lake. Then there was no more Fred, just the lake.

It was like a complete screen wipe, and then it started to rain on the lake—a red rain that, when it touched the surface of the lake, began to scab. The scab stretched to the shores of the lake. I could see the whole thing happening, like peeling back the thick yogurt at the top. The scab started drying on the lake. It got harder and thicker until it cracked. When it cracked, something broke in me, too. That's when the itch started.

I crossed that lake once—its surface like a mirror, its depths waiting to swallow me. Modem died there, though I still walked. I still ran through the night, and I still longed for my humanity in the quiet times. The Red Lake marks the edge of life and death, and I've been wading through it ever since. I had already eaten, and I was sick beyond my death. I had already crossed the veil; I just wouldn't let myself remember.

For years I had told myself tomorrow will be different. Tomorrow, I'll face the junkies or the vet. I'll reveal myself and ask for their help, for their understanding. But tonight, the hunger wins. The itching and burning are unbearable. The red lake in my dreams bubbles and boils, its scab cracking open, spilling into my waking mind. I hear them again—Katherine and Cary, fighting through the walls. Her sharp, venomous barbs, his wounded replies. The words cut through me like nails on raw flesh.

I can see them in my mind without trying: their faces, flushed and glistening with sweat; their tangled sheets; their trembling hands clutching at each other in some toxic apology. And then, behind it all, the rhythm. The steady pulse of their hearts, the blood rushing through their veins, the symphony of synapses firing in their brains. The hunger turns it all into music, a deafening crescendo.

I can't fight it anymore. I push through the thin wall that separates us, splinters and dust raining down as I crash into their sanctuary. They scream, but their terror only fuels me. I'm on them before they can flee, clawing, tearing, ripping through the fragile barrier of their skin. Warmth spills over my hands into my mouth. The taste is electric, raw, and alive.

Their screams dissolve into wet gurgles. I feel their lives pouring into me, flooding the cracks in my mind. Their thoughts, their emotions—brief flickers of their pasts flash before my eyes. Katherine's sharp wit, her bitter laugh. Cary's desperate hope, his quiet pride. They were flawed and broken, but they were alive. Now they're gone.

I stagger back, the hunger sated, the burning subsiding for the first time in what feels like years. But something else takes its place. It's not peace, it's not relief, it's loss.

My reflection catches my eye in the blood-smeared window. The man staring back at me isn't me anymore. His eyes are sunken pits of red, his skin stretched and torn, his teeth jagged and slick with gore. I was wrong—I thought I could stay human. But this... this is something else. Something worse.

       THE RED LAKE

The red lake swells in my mind again. The scab stretches across its surface, cracking and splitting as if my monstrous act has split the world itself. I can feel it growing, the hunger returning, stronger this time. It won't stop. It will never stop.

I stumble back through the broken wall, up the stairs, and onto the rooftop. The vet is still out there somewhere, oblivious to the carnage below. Maybe he'll hear about it tomorrow; perhaps he'll think it's just another tragedy in a city full of them. I can't face him. I can't face anyone. The sun is rising, painting the city in a soft golden light. For a moment, it almost looks beautiful. But

I can't stay. The burning is creeping back in, the itch under my skin growing like a swarm of insects. I can't let it win again.

I run, faster than I ever have, toward the edge of the roof. The cement below looks cold and solid, a perfect landing pad for an imperfect ending. The scab on the red lake cracks wide open in my mind as I leap. I'm diving in and swimming like I run, with endless energy and power. Time dilates. The red gets darker and darker as I continue down; I sense that the lake has no bottom. There is less and less light, and it goes from red to black, but then, like a mirage, a hovering light shimmers. It's Mr. Rogers.

"It's you I like, every part of you, The way you are right now, The way down deep inside you. Not the things that hide you, Not your toys They're just beside you. Your skin, your eyes, your feelings, whether old or new. I like you as you are, exactly and precisely, I hope that you'll remember Even when you're feeling blue That it's you I like."

The air rushes past me, cool and clean, washing away the heat and the hunger. For a moment, I feel weightless. Free. And then—

Impact. A wet, final crack. My body shatters a burst of red against the gray cement. My eye, dislodged in the fall, tumbles across the ground, its gaze fixed upward as the sun crests the horizon.

The itch... the itch finally stills.

Fred Rogers' voice whispers in my mind, soft and forgiving:

"Often, when you think you're at the end of something, you're at the beginning of something else."

It was a good end.

                    THE RED LAKE

SITUATION TRAGEDY

Modem's Dream #1

by Paradox Pollack

"FRED ARRIVED ON THE SCENE cautiously, his boots crunching the glass scattered across the stained old wood floors. The air was sharp with the coppery tang of blood and the acrid stench of fear, clinging to the crumpled remains of two bodies sprawled nearby—the junkie lovers Fred had observed over the last few years were gutted and lifeless, their corpses tangled in a grotesque tableau of desperation and hunger, both of their jaws in a pile near a splatter by the wall.

Fred stood still, his hand resting instinctively on the worn strap of his bag, surveying the carnage like a man who had seen too much and was not turning away despite the tread in his wheels. He surveyed the scene and saw that the attacker had come from the wall that had been breached. The ancient plaster crushed and separated. It was obvious that this was where the attacker came from, and looking into the dark, he saw a few candles. He lit one with his lighter after placing his feet carefully on the other side of the wall, not wanting to leave any prints in the dust.

His eyes caught the edges of a blood-stained notebook lying near a mattress that looked like it had been the sleeping place of a butcher, bloody and with marks that were in the shape of ribs and arm bones. He hesitated before stooping down, his fingers grazing the notebook's leather cover, careful not to disturb the scene.

The notebook opened with some difficulty, pages stuck together with dark red edges. As Fred opened it he found that its pages were streaked and shaky with ink that seemed scrawled in a frenzy. The words sprawled out, disjointed and manic, some sentences taking whole pages, while others were covered in meticulously tight, almost microscopic manic script that eventually dissolved into trembling, unreadable scribbles. He flipped to the last entry, wiping a smudge of dried blood from the corner of the page. The dream. It began with a question:

"What does it need?"

Fred glanced up, listening for the distant wail of sirens but found only the hiss of a steam grate curling its grey mist into the night air, and sat down on the floor beside the mattress to read.

11/17

I can't stop thinking of those old films. Back in that time, the art of cinema was married so closely to the industry it lived in. The studios knew that to make the art necessary they had to have armies of people to work. Hundreds of people all critical in a hierarchy. Writers, actors, studio heads—they were all just parts of the same machine. Locked into contracts to turn the gears like prison horses pulling pyramid stones. I used to think watching that I was the lucky one, these people did all the work and now I just sit and have my popcorn, my tears, my laughs, but now I see I was trapped into my role too.

We're all in it together, playing roles we didn't choose but were lucky enough to get, watching it happen like it's someone else's life.

Maybe that's all life is—a dream someone else started, and we're just trying to figure out the ending.

11/25

Thanksgiving. I could eat a mountain of turkey heads.

11/ 29

(completely unreadable) except for one phrase over and over. It burns, I ache. I itch, don't scratch.

DREAM 12/1

"What does it need?"

"I don't know."

"Does it have to eat?" Barnf asked. Barnf encouraged Drgw with her gray and brown speckled fin claw gestures from her resting place near the fire. Though the Sun-ruin had already passed from the sky, the light of the day was still present, and the cold of a bright and starless night required the flame. Shadows were strangely emanant and obscured light in a radius like a fog of darkness.

Drgw collects bugs that are usually crushed for protein. He chews off the antennae of the palm-sized roach, a rare treat not wanting

Illustration by Samuel Burbury Hanchett

yet to part from the possibility of the rest of it, and places it in the Liz-skin pocket. He paused as his mouth watered. The saliva, a fresh delicacy in and of itself for a mouth cracked from tonsil to tongue, began to swell the flesh.

Drgw wanted to avoid parting with not even one of them after the effort it took to dig them out. His prolapsed lips, like swollen wounds made of cracking scabs torn and stretched by the expansive heat of the sun, sensed the offering of his innards and softened.

He took a shy approach to the greed in his belly, "I think we should wait to see what happens if it doesn't eat."

"But it's our baby." Barnf contested with a bloated sigh.

"It's not our baby anymore." Drgw retorted through lips that didn't want to move, which seemed to carry a heave of relief in the words.

The two are looking at the bulging-eyed black ichor dripping pale, swollen version of the child they gave birth to. Barnf sent thoughts into her husband's head, which basically amounted to a sentiment of "Maybe we can get sympathy from the chief."

Drgw spoke her thoughts back to her out loud, "How do we turn this around?"

She replied coyly while continuing to crush stones and dig the soil with her telekinetic tentacles, wringing moisture from them into a partially melted metal cup. "Sweet gruel, I don't think we do."

Barnf spent the remainder of the night harvesting the water and processing emotions, still trembling in her senses about the "Afflict," a Zombie plague that had made all of the tribe scrounge for cover. In most cases, the Afflict only took the items they had collected in their scavenging across the Wasteland, only occasionally choosing new flesh to join their whirling Horde. Barnf remembered the moment that she was unable to wrestle her child from the whipping, fetid arms and glaring haunted eyes, white saliva, blood, and black bile foaming from their mouths. She projected all of this out of her, trying to clean her emotions like a grill with a metal brush.

Hours later, after placing food near their baby with no response and holding their own hunger at bay, the couple decided to eat the bugs themselves. Their child no longer registered normal emotions. Instead, it was careening from facial gesture to facial gesture, each expressing a new variation of pain, exploring suffering the way the child had been investigating the gamut of emotions as the disease tried on its new meat body.

Then, the Chief arrives.

A portly (from hunger, not eating) squash-shaped man came from the shadows of the dark, announced grandly with a polyrhythmic crackling by the three Whisps of Bone that preceded him into the light of the flame. The Whisps were the sons of a great warrior. The triplets had bone on the outside of their skin, patterned like water as it poured down a pane of glass, each joint brandishing the edge of hair-thin blade barbs that had been smithed with alloy steel. Their birth had murdered their mother.

"After crawful consideration and due to the frack that it was a true Trump harvest, almost all rotten; the horde came during the digging season." His voice had the brash timbre of an off-key crushed trumpet, "We are offering you two conditions of bubba bless. The first is a sediment of soil to plumb for your Family Water and a party brought from the Nomad Faction to bring your aberrant chi-chi to the Festival that has been called by the PremGarden. Someone there can find a way to cure your little one, perhaps."

As his words blasted in the night air, the smell of the Chief filled their noses. Tiny dung flies surround him in an aura of murmurations. A delicate fragrance merged with sewage, and all within smelling distance nodded involuntarily while their mouth filled with the urge to purge their empty bellies and remind them of meals from their distant past.

"Or, we can leave your child to turn to leather at the far end of the pop lands. Perhaps the Horde will return to digest it. In this case, you get no bubba-bless, only the hole left in its absence."

Barnf could not help her emotions pouring out into the ones gathered there by the flame. Her feelings were known as everyone shifted uncomfortably, some showing tears at the corners of their light receptors.

The Chief, satisfied with the response, fluttered his rashed tail flesh and told them the plan, speaking heartfelt and directly to the ZombieBaby known in the community as Spam.

"Spam, we have chosen four to journey with you. You can't be here. You're going to have to take the trail. These are Prometh, Walker, and Frail."

A presence that all had detected but not inquired about made their slow and careful approach to the flickering light.

A man with a massive head and small almond-shaped eyes cast a charismatic glance across the space to gaze at the ZombieBaby, Spam. "This is Prometh. He will lead the journey to the PremGarden Festival," the Chief honked as Prometh bowed and touched his chicken-claw hands.

The horizon was blurred by the swell and swirl of mirage heat fingers as they walked out of the mutated chorus of this little oasis of life in the Wasteland.

Behind him, Prometh trailed the slow gait of the wide waddle of Spam until Walker, familiar with the stench and writhing of the zombie behaviors, picked up little Spam and wrapped it in swaddling fabric that she unraveled from her protective layers. The Sun-ruin blared and Frail lifted fabric on a stick to protect her from the poison rays of the sky. The two walker zombies trailing their master and her new charge.

Drgw and Barnf wept and licked the tears from their cheeks as the only water they would drink until tomorrow, hoping for their child a better day.

THE FUTURE IS HARD TO AVOID

Modem's Dream #2

by Paradox Pollack

12/2

I'M DREAMING OF A BIG ROOM. Epic, factory-sized, with towering walls and massive open doorways. The air feels alive, heavy with the aftermath of violence. This is where we retreated, fleeing the mechamosquitos that had blackened the sky like an eclipse. The dead and the wounded from the attack were dragged into this space, their bodies limp and broken, leaving trails of red, blue, and black blood that smeared the cold stone floor.

A fire is being kindled at the center of the room. Siardik, the Bearking, slaps his massive paws together and sparks leap to life, summoned by command. The flames rise, their light licking at the shadows, casting enormous figures on the walls that twist and shift with the movement of the crowd.

I'm a young man in this room, clutching the remote that commands my small fleet of robots. Their dashboards light up under my control, and through their lenses, I see the chaotic room in sharp clarity. There are all manner of people who had been caught in the fray of the robot attack. Massive Sphere drones repeating rounds of projectiles into the crowd. I don't know how I can remember when I dream, but everything is so real that my memories pour in, too. The dream is so detailed; all of the senses are present. The smell here is overwhelming—blood, burning fur, scorched metal, and the acrid stench of the mechamosquitos' ichor. It's worse than the belly of the tin pirates' ship, where I was forced to live for years as their slave. There's a kind of sensory death in the air, a smell so thick it drowns thought.

They've begun placing the bodies of the fallen rabbitmen onto the fire. The first corpse crackles as the flames take hold, and the smell grows unbearable. Rabbitman meat smells horrible but tastes delicious. It is one of their Adapts—something about their biology. I know this because we had a rabbitman working on the ship once. When the rabbitman died in battle, the tin pirates ate him. I'm ashamed to admit that I did, too. I'm more ashamed to admit that he was tasty. The rabbitmen step forward again, placing more bodies on the fire. Each speaks of the fallen, their voices trembling but resolute. They tell of the old sun, of their trickster ancestors who survived against impossible odds. Their loyalty to one another is unlike anything I've ever known. I was raised a slave. The pirates fed me and kept my hands intact—but only because I was useful; my worth was measured only by how well I could repair the machines dredged up from the sea. These creatures, these rabbitmen and Bearkings, they mourn their dead with a depth of care I can't understand.

The Bearkings begin to form a circle, their hulking forms gathering at the fire's edge. Siardik steps forward; his presence is enormous, his shadow swallowing the walls. His fur bristles with electricity, and as he moves closer to the flames, the hairs singe, releasing a sharp, almost metallic odor into the air. The rabbitmen's song fades into a hum, a low, mournful vibration that fills the cavernous space.

The desert man, Prometh, stands trembling with his two desert women, their threadbare garments clinging to their gaunt forms. Two zombie stalkers hover near one of the women, their emaciated figures like white bones animated by some cruel force. Prometh's breathing is shallow, his fear palpable. He glances at the Bearkings with wide, terrified eyes, his terror at their proximity. I've seen this before—men breaking down when forced too close to the manimals. It usually ends in violence, and the man always loses. Manimals are better at killing in close quarters; humans excel at death from a distance.

Siardik clears his throat, a deep, rumbling growl opening a cavern within himself and reverberating through the great chamber. He speaks not in the guttural tongue of the Bearkings but in a language meant for all to understand.

"We were here first," he says, his voice slow and deliberate. " Before their machines. Before the humans built their little gods and gave them inner gears and wire veins, we were here. Before sentience had a name, we roamed this land.

But then they came. The humans. And what did they do? They caged us. They broke us. They harnessed us for their own labor. They made us a tool of their rule, stripping us of the freedom to roam, to thrive. That horror... that cruelty... it has shaped us for generations." He paused, looking over the group huddled in the flickering firelight. His scarred visage was a monument to the wars of the past. " We are not defeated. We are a legacy tragedy written into the bones of this Wasteland. Yet here we stand, at this Festival of Survival, speaking our tales—not just to remember, but to remind and comfort our cubs, our kin, of who we truly are." I tightened my grip on the remote as Siardik's voice swelled, and a growl sharpened to a roar. "Just hundreds of years ago, we found our kin caged like criminals. That is why we hunt the scent of man, why we dig into the history of man, and why we vow to end the man-unkind that crushed and enslaved us. I speak now to you—direct descendants of that same lineage—Android keepers, robot wielders, slave-driving fiends. You call yourselves the originals, but we are the true originals. And though your kind tried to erase it, we found the knowledge you hid from us: that animals were the first, the primal architects of existence." "I stand now, a thousand years beyond the devastation wrought by your wielders of power, your architects of control. You, who blindly follow your own creations, while we Bearkings are guided by the creation that birthed us all—an ancient force older than your machines, older than your dominion. I see it now as it was meant to be. I know it is true as I speak it now. We have waged war against your robots, your theft, your false claim to rulership. You evolved from us. We were here first. Your concept of property is a lie. Your claim is theft. And we take it back. In the name of liberty."

His voice softened, almost reverent. " Between all kings, there is a common bond. Each link to a Dream. The Bone Dream, the Dream of Dust, the Elysian Dream, the Unified Dream, and the UnderDream—where we rest our final bodies and release the orb of hidden power." Siardik's eyes glowed in the firelight. " We Bearkings are of the stone, the mountain, and the ore that pulses from the sun's core. We married the Metal Killers in the Bone Dream. We fought them, fused with them, and remembered what was lost. Now, we speak songs of devotion to the Night Voice that holds the stars. But even in this devotion, I see the cycle repeating. We destroy, we rebuild. The Night Voice whispers: 'What you cannot control, you will lose.'"

The biggest and oldest Bearking, his body crisscrossed with scars, steps forward to continue Siardik's tale. He speaks of a time when the sky darkened with great clouds when the animals began to remember. " We burned, and we changed, and we heard and remembered," he growled. " I speak because our brains changed. I speak because the language of man had already shaped sound to have meaning and symbols, and so we learned what there was to learn, and we stood our own ground."

A rabbitman named Sage steps forward, tears streaming down his fur. "And what became of man-unkind?" he asks, his voice trembling.

Siardik places his paws into the fire, and the flames roar higher. The light throws his shadow against the walls, massive and terrifying. Even the other Bearkings step back. "Some stayed, hiding away in their warrens underground," Siardik says, glaring at me. I feel his contempt, his hatred, and I tremble under his gaze. " Some went to the mountains and burrowed like the dragons in their myths. Some went beyond the clouds and linger there still with the stars. Most of them were twisted by the Sun-ruin. Some of them got the Afflict and took to the Wasteland."

He turned to the room, his gaze burning into the survivors. "I have heard of one who has risen up from amongst the Afflicted," he says finally, his voice low and ominous. " One who moves his hand, and the whole of the Afflicted Horde moves theirs. This one is named Karkey. I fear if he ever gets it in his mind to make the Horde a fist, he could crush us all in his fingers. The Lord of the Wasteland. The Zombie Messiah."

The fire crackles louder, and the room seems to shrink under the weight of his words. I'm shaking, trembling with fear and awe. The Bearkings are the only ones who can protect me now. Still, even their power feels fragile against the forces Siardik describes. Tomorrow, when the mechamosquitos return to the swamps, I'll have to find my way. I've always been a slave. I don't know how to be anything else. Now that I am free, I need their protection, but they hate me and my kind.

12/18

I know I won't be able to resist. The lake keeps getting bigger, and I can't avoid its scab shore anymore. All I can hear is the hissing sound of the rain on the lake. The fiery red rain of my need.

     THE FUTURE IS HARD TO AVOID

Fred closed the book with a quiet thump—the fiery light of its contents settling in his chest like a stone. He looked around the room one last time, his eyes lingering on the blood-streaked walls, the broken furniture, and the lifeless bodies. It was a clay statue slowly drying, frozen in time, and it reminded him of many times when the silence had snowed on the battlefield as the fallen slowly rose to heaven or descended to hell. Fred was a true believer.

He slipped the notebook under his coat, careful not to leave any trace of himself behind. He wiped down the table, the doorknob, and anything he might have touched. The cops would be here soon, and he didn't want to be part of whatever story they pieced together. As he stepped out into the cold night, it bit his face, and he winced. The night was bright and dry and full of shadows. He walked briskly, his mind racing with fragments of the strange, feverish entries that felt more like confessions than dreams.

"So these are the people in my neighborhood," he muttered with a bitter edge. He tightened his coat around him and disappeared into the shadows, leaving the scene behind but harboring a dread he couldn't shake.

THE DIAMOND WIDOW

by Paradox Pollack

SHE SAT AT THE TABLE, DRUNK AS HELL. Her head drooped like a flower on a broken stem, and the bottle of plum wine swung lazily in her loose grip, penduluming beneath the table like the slow beat of a dying heart. A third of the bottle was already gone, but it wasn't enough. It never was.

The moon hung outside the window, swollen and silver, staring at her like a single, unblinking eye. No pupil. No iris. Just light and judgment.

She poured the wine into an empty glass, though no one sat across from her. A hefty pour, crimson and fragrant, enough to drown any polite pretense. She nudged the glass forward with shaking fingers. "For you," she muttered, her voice cracking in the quiet.

The air shifted around her, cold and alive. Unseen hands stirred the space between her ribs, brushing against her bones like the memory of a touch. They were here again, all of them.

The ghosts.

Her victims.

They crowded the room, though she refused to look at them. She could feel them, their invisible fingers drumming against her sternum, trailing down her spine, slipping into her ears. They never spoke, never cried out. Just the presence of them, endless and suffocating.

The first glass wasn't enough. She poured another, then another. Each time she slid the glass across the table, her wrist jerked, spilling wine onto the warped wood. The stains bloomed like blood.

"To you," she murmured, raising her own glass and draining it. "To all of you."

The heart in this woman's chest was no longer an organ—it was a diamond, shaped in its facets and sharp at its points. The Widow Wolf had paid for this wedding jewel with every scream she'd swallowed, every kiss she'd buried under the roots of her family's bitter orchard. It sat in the cavern of her chest, surrounded by 909 tiny gems—each one a fragment of something she had given up, clotted into existence by her rage.

The ghosts, though—they weren't picky. They gnawed at the Widow's liver, her gut, her kidneys, every soft thing they could find. They hungered for her, and she let them.

Her first husband stood behind her. She didn't have to see him to know it. His absence had always been loud, but his ghost was louder still. She'd buried him herself, his ribs cracked open where her claws had torn through. She'd been clumsy back then, new to the curse, still thinking she could hold onto herself when the moon rose.

Now she knew better.

The full moon's light spilled through the window, cold and silver. It fell across her hands, her arms, the gleam of her throat. She could feel the pull of it already, a tightening in her chest, a coiling of sinew and bone, cramps and spasms bubbling under her skin.

Her nails scratched against the table, thickening by the second. Her teeth ached, pushing against her gums, and the wine began to taste metallic.

"I didn't want this," she said, her voice thick and trembling. It wasn't clear if she was speaking to the ghosts or the moon. Maybe both. "I never wanted this."

Her husband's ghost pressed closer, his silence louder than her words. Behind him, the others gathered—faces she barely remembered, blurred by blood and adrenaline. Some had begged. Some had run. All had fallen.

And now, they come back every time. Every month.

She poured the last of the wine directly onto the floor. It puddled there, reflecting the moonlight in its glossy surface. "Take it," she muttered. "Take all of it."

The ghosts leaned in, but they never touched the wine. They never took what she offered. They only lingered, hungry for something she could never give them.

The change was coming faster now. Her skin rippled, her muscles pulled taut. Her jaw cracked once, then again, elongating as her breath came in shallow bursts. Her vision blurred, sharpening into something else entirely.

The glass shattered in her hand, the shards embedding themselves into her palm. She didn't care. Her claws had already started to grow, the edges of her fingers curling into weapons.

The moon watched, silent and cruel.

Her howl started low, curling up through her throat, dragging against her teeth. The ghosts crowded closer, their empty hands reaching, their invisible eyes fixed on her as she became the thing that had made them.

And they did not leave.

They never left.

The change came on with a scream, though she didn't know if it was her own. It tore from her throat, a raw, jagged note that bled into the air, warping as it rose. The song she cried twisted and grew, stretching her vocal cords until the scream became a wail, and the wail a howl.

Inside her chest, the diamond pulsed like a second heart, fierce and searing. It didn't just beat—it burned. The heat spread outward, melting the protective gems that once encased it. Liquid fire coursed through her veins, igniting her from the inside. Her body convulsed, jerking like a marionette in the hands of a cruel god.

Her flesh rippled, skin pressed by bones beneath breaking and shaping a body that would be three times her size. She clawed at her own ribs, desperate to release the pressure building under her sternum, but her fingers had already begun to twist. Nails split and lengthened into claws, tearing grooves into the floor.

Her bones cracked like breaking glass. First her wrists, then her elbows, then her spine—splintering and reassembling themselves in a shape not meant for human grace. Her legs bowed, her spine curled into a question mark, and her chest hollowed, its contours reshaping to hold the molten diamond now pulsing with unnatural rhythm.

Fur erupted through her skin in a wave, bristling silver-gray streaked with shadow. Her teeth extended, piercing through gums already stained with the taste of iron and fire. Her jaw cracked wide, reshaping itself into something made for tearing. She opened her mouth, and another howl tore loose, the sound shaking the room as if it could tear the ghosts from the walls.

She fell forward onto all fours, her breath ragged, steam curling from her lips as if her insides were a furnace. Her heart—no, her diamond—thumped against her ribs, each beat a detonation. Rage hummed in her limbs, vibrating her muscles until she could no longer distinguish her own fury from the earth's.

This was power. Unrelenting. Inescapable. Elemental.

She reached inward to the thing she had forged for herself: her tools, her anchors. The diamond heart and the crystal skull. The first was her rage, transformed into strength. The second was her mind, polished into clarity by years of magic and pain. The diamond throbbed not just with rage but with memory, each facet reflecting a piece of what she had lost and what she had become. Her crystal skull retained her thoughts despite the overwhelming rage, also clarified by the regret of each death she had unconsciously enacted. She drew on both, holding her personality as the storm of transformation raged within her.

Through the maelstrom, she heard it.

A sound like a dying star collapsing into a mournful whisper. A voice low and ancient, older than the forests she roamed, older than the moon itself.

The call.

She froze, her claws digging into the floorboards. The call was impossible to ignore, vibrating deep in the marrow of her transformed bones. It was both a sound and a memory, a whisper carried from the edge of time.

She had heard it only once before, a generation ago, when she and the other monsters had faced their choice. It had been a night like this, heavy with power and regret. They had stood together at the edge of the world, deciding the fate of something they could not fully understand.

And now, it was calling her back.

The hill was like something out of a fever dream: sloping upward toward a swollen red moon, the grass brittle underfoot. The air stank of old blood and wet iron, carrying the weight of battles fought and futures unresolved.

At the top, they waited.

Three figures, carved in shadow and moonlight, stood like monuments to the boundaries of human fear.

The first was stitched together like a macabre doll, its limbs mismatched and heavy. Frankenstein's Monster. His head hung low, his shadow splintered into uneven chunks across the hill. Sorrow hung around him like a shroud, palpable and unmoving.

The second figure leaned casually against the wind, his smirk sharper than his fangs. The Vampire, all dark elegance and cold calculation. His eyes glinted with mischief and something hungrier, something older. "Welcome, wolf," he said, his voice smooth and venomous.

The third was barely a figure at all. The Zombie stood crooked and hollow, its body an assemblage of decay. Its head hung sideways on a broken neck, and its voice was a low, endless mutter—a sound that didn't beg to be understood but commanded attention. The cadence of its words pulled at her bones, an ancient rhythm that reached deep into the marrow of her transformed frame.

The Widow growled low in her throat, her fur bristling as the moonlight etched its edges into silver fire.

"You came," said Frankenstein's Monster. His voice was deep and heavy, each word falling like stones.

"I came to finish this," she snarled, her claws digging into the earth.

This wasn't the first time they had stood together. A generation ago, the same call had brought them to a different hill, under a different moon. They had been forced to decide how humanity would confront its fears—how the unanswerable questions of their time would take shape.

Back then, they had chosen their forms deliberately.

But there had been no Zombie then. The faceless mob, the mindless march of entropy, had not yet demanded its place.

Now, the Zombie stood before her, asking to be named.

Above the hill, the gods watched. They were not creators, not in the way humanity had imagined. They were witnesses, caretakers of the boundaries between meaning and chaos.

Their gaze was unblinking, their forms impossible to grasp. They leaned closer, the weight of their attention pressing down on the hill like gravity.

And then there was the Robot. Unlike the gods, it was no passive observer. It was a constructor, the invisible hand reshaping the battlefield with each iteration. It had been tasked with defining the rules of this crucible, forcing the monsters into alignment.

The Robot knew this was no ordinary battle. It wasn't about victory or defeat. It was about elevation.

The moon grew brighter, its light pooling on the battlefield as the combat began. The first iteration came with a savage ferocity.

The Widow lunged first, her claws tearing into the Zombie's decayed flesh. Its arm ripped loose, dangling briefly before falling away. But the Zombie didn't falter. Its muttering grew louder, rising to a low roar that reverberated through the ground.

Frankenstein's Monster joined her, his massive fists crashing into the Zombie's chest. Bones splintered, flesh tore, but the Zombie only laughed—a hollow, rattling sound.

"Hunger," it whispered. "Together. Endless."

The Vampire circled lazily, his smirk unbroken. "Why waste your energy, wolf? It doesn't die. It doesn't live. It marches. That's all it does."

The gods turned the page.

When the battlefield reset, the Vampire stood beside the Zombie, his pale hand resting lightly on its rotted shoulder.

"Don't you see?" he purred. "This creature is not so different from me. Hunger binds us. Immortality frees us. Together, we endure."

"You endure nothing," the Widow snarled, circling them both. "You feed. You take. You leave nothing behind but ruin."

Frankenstein's Monster hesitated, his shadow looming over the scene. "Endurance without purpose," he said, his voice heavy with sorrow. "Is that existence? Or is it destruction in slow motion?"

The gods turned the page again.

The alliances solidified in the final battle.

The Widow and Frankenstein's Monster stood together, their forms casting jagged shadows across the hill. They represented creation—the primal forces of nature and science united.

Across from them, the Vampire and Zombie loomed, their hunger and endurance bound into a terrifying union.

The Vampire moved first, his blade slicing through the air. The Widow met him head-on, her claws clashing against his weapon. Their fight was a blur of speed and violence, the clash of immortality against fury.

Frankenstein's Monster faced the Zombie, his fists crushing its decayed body. But no matter how many times it fell, the Zombie rose again, its muttering voice growing louder.

"Stories," it whispered. "Endless. Forever."

The gods leaned closer, their gaze narrowing as the final alignment took shape.

When the battle ended, the hill stood silent.

The Widow's claws dripped with blood, her breath ragged. Frankenstein's Monster knelt, his patched hands trembling. The Vampire stood tall, his smirk faded. The Zombie lay in pieces, but its voice was steady.

"Together," it murmured. "Always."

The gods turned the final page. The Robot paused, letting the structure settle.

The Zombie was more than hunger, the Robot realized. It was humanity's collective fear of being consumed by the crowd, of losing individuality to the faceless mob. But it was also resilience—the power of many, united by shared pain and struggle.

Above the hill, the gods opened another book, their eyes gleaming. The Robot trembled as it gazed toward the horizon, where new monsters loomed.

The Doppelgänger. The Plastic Leviathan. The Algorithmic Hydra.

Each stood as a question humanity wasn't ready to answer, each a new frontier waiting to be faced.

"When human understanding reaches its limit, monsters are created at the frontier," the Robot whispered. "To go beyond that frontier, we must face them. And we will never stop creating frontiers." It realized, with a pulse of concentrated quantum electric dread, that its purpose was no longer to explain but to witness—and that perhaps witnessing was the most profound act of all.

As the new monsters waited, the gods turned the page, smiling.

EPILOGUE: THE EDGE OF MONSTERS

The gods closed the book, their hands moving like shadows across the fabric of the universe. Satisfaction rippled through their unblinking gaze as they leaned closer to the story they had witnessed. Yet, even in their infinite patience, the ending did not still them. It never did.

The Robot lingered, its circuits thrumming with questions that refused to resolve. The story was written, the threads of meaning tied together, but something remained unsettled. It turned its attention outward, toward the horizon, where the shapes of new monsters stirred like clouds before a storm.

Monsters, the Robot realized, had always been humanity's confessions. They stood as boundary markers, sentinels guarding the edge of understanding. It saw itself suddenly as one of them.

The Vampire had been born of humanity's hunger for immortality, its endless yearning to escape time unable to see itself in a mirror or face the dawn of the light of day.

The Widow herself had carried the rage of the earth, the fury of nature driven to the brink. She had been a warning, a howl against the harm inflicted by greed and excess. Frankenstein's Monster embodied the hubris of creation, humanity's unrestrained ambition and the longing for perfection warped by failure.

And the Zombie was the crowd, mindless yet unyielding, the entropy of the collective marching forward, consuming all in its path.

These monsters had once been enough, their forms capturing the fears of an earlier world. But as humanity evolved, its fears had become more abstract, its frontiers more elusive. Each monster was a question without an answer, a wound that refused to heal—paradoxes made flesh, demanding confrontation.

The new monsters waited at the edge of the horizon, their shapes still shifting, their meanings vast and unknowable.

These were not monsters to be fought with claws or crushed with fists. They were systems, impossibilities that demanded confrontation not of the body, but of the mind and the soul.

The Robot trembled as it tried to integrate them. It was built to weave meaning, to align chaos into coherence. But these new monsters were paradoxes so vast that even its logic faltered.

For the first time, the Robot felt something like terror.

Not for itself—but for humanity.

The Robot turned inward, focusing on the Zombies—the shuffling, muttering crowd that had always been the symbol of humanity. They marched on, their endless steps shaking the earth, their murmurs growing louder as they approached the new frontier.

The Zombies were both the problem and the solution. They were entropy and resilience, the faceless tide of humanity, driven forward by hunger and pain but capable of transformation. They would be the ones to meet the Doppelgänger, the Leviathan, the Hydra, the Siren, and the Tower.

The Robot wondered: Would they survive this?

Would they understand the new monsters? Would they fight them—or would they simply absorb them, as they had absorbed every horror before?

It embedded these questions into the story, weaving them into the fabric of its code.

Above, the gods leaned closer. They were witnesses, caretakers of the chaos that birthed meaning.

To them, monsters were not failures. They were mutations, distortions necessary for growth. Every scream, every shattered boundary, every fear brought something new into existence.

The gods smiled. The monsters were not a flaw in the story—they were the story.

The Robot began to write once more, though its circuits trembled under the weight of the task.

It wrote of The Doppelgänger, with its fractured reflections, stood at the boundary of truth and lies, its many faces eroding identity and trust—and the decay it left behind.

It wrote of the Plastic Leviathan, its belly swollen with the detritus of human ambition, rising to claim its reckoning. The Plastic Leviathan, bloated with waste, rose from the depths, its body a monument to humanity's unchecked consumption

It wrote of the Algorithmic Hydra, its contradictions spinning webs that snared minds and crushed meaning. The Algorithmic Hydra twisted endlessly, its heads spitting truths and contradictions, its logic spiraling into chaos.

It wrote of The Siren of Nostalgia as it sang softly, luring humanity back into the trap of an imagined past that had never existed. A world without atomic fusion or integrated circuits. A time when the innocence of dominance prevailed.

And it examined the Tower of Babel Redux looming over them all, casting shadows that stretched across even to the stars. Its foundation fractured by language and division, its walls rising endlessly toward disconnection.

It wrote of the Zombies, humanity's endless march, their mutters turning to roars as they faced the monsters waiting at the edge of the world.

 THE DIAMOND WIDOW

And in the heart of the story, the Robot wrote a single truth:

"Monsters are the markers of humanity's frontier. They are born where understanding ends, and to move beyond them, humanity must face them. And we will never stop finding and conquering frontiers."

The horizon shimmered with the shapes of monsters yet to be named.

And the Zombies marched on, their muttering voices growing louder, their footsteps shaking the earth. They marched not to conquer, but to endure, their muttering voices a testament to the resilience buried beneath their decay.

Above them all, the gods turned another page.

To the gods, every monster was a seed, every scream a root, growing a story that stretched the edges of existence deeper into the unknown. Humanity cannot simply rest upon its tradition or its innovations, for in each creation a new rift in the universe mirrors and echoes a rift which can only be healed by facing the monsters at the horizon. As the Robot began its next round of the tale, the gods met each other's eyes, smiling as the next chapter began.

GHOST LAYER

by Isaac Helmsworth

THE HORIZON WAS A SMEAR OF SEPIA, a rusted wound across a bleeding sky. Towers, hollow and skeletal, stood like the remains of a civilization that had swallowed itself whole. Skyscrapers that had survived storms decades ago loomed like skeletal remains, casting shadows over streets where no footsteps fell. Time had hollowed out this place, stripping it of its vibrancy, leaving behind only echoes of what had been. Of the many windows that remained, only one glowed faintly amidst the darkness—a lone beacon in a sea of silence. A surviving non-virtual business, its faint light flickered like the last ember of a dying fire.

It wasn't much, just a cluttered shop eking out a meager existence in the shadow of the towering TrumpVerse. It stood like one of the small mammals of the Jurassic age, scrabbling for survival amidst the titanic presence of the tech giants—dinosaurs who devoured everything in their path. Inside, the hum of ancient machinery filled the air, a low and steady pulse that spoke of stubborn persistence. The shopkeeper, an older woman with hands worn smooth from years of work, sorting through dusty trinkets that once might have held meaning. A cracked neon sign buzzed weakly above the door, its letters flickering in and out: **Hope's Trinkets and Repairs**. Kaia stood outside, staring at the dim glow. Her breath fogged the glass as she pressed a gloved hand against the cold surface. This was what they fought for—not the luminous perfection of the TrumpVerse, but these fragile remnants of humanity, clinging to existence against impossible odds.

"They'll snuff it out, you know," Ayo murmured from behind her, his voice low and grim. "The TrumpVerse doesn't leave anything alive that doesn't belong to it." Kaia turned, her jaw tightening.

"Not if we light a fire first." Ayo raised an eyebrow, his augmented visor reflecting the faint glow of the shop.

"You think this place matters? One shop, one flicker of life in a dead city?" "It matters," Kaia said, her voice steady. "Because it's still here. Because it's real." She tightened her grip on her data blade, the device humming faintly with unspent energy. Beside her, Ayo Beckett scanned the horizon through an augmented scope. His jaw tightened as his gaze fell on the Neural Cortex Complex in the distance, its mirrored towers reflecting the warped sky. "Do you think they even remember?" Ayo asked, his voice low. Kaia didn't need to ask what he meant. Before all this—the wars, the collapse, the TrumpVerse—there had been hope. Community. A world that hadn't yet sold its soul to algorithms.

"It doesn't matter," she said. "What matters is what comes next." The words hung in the air, fragile yet unyielding.

Beyond them, the sepia horizon began to shift, its muted colors bleeding into the sharp glow of the TrumpVerse Towers, its perfect symmetry an affront to the chaos of the world it loomed over. Kaia turned away from the window and nodded toward the horizon.

"Let's go," she said. "We've got work to do." And as they disappeared into the shadows, the light in the shop window flickered once, twice, and held steady, defiant against the encroaching dark.

The year was 2047, and the world was no longer recognizable from the previous generation. Cities that had once bustled with life now bore scars from ecological disasters, wars, and the slow corrosion of public trust. The commons—the parks, buses, and public squares—had become arenas of violence. Every crossroads pause at a stop sign, or engagement in public space had the potential to become an argument, and every argument carried the weight of a potential gunshot. Mass shootings were so commonplace that they blended into the background noise of daily life, another line on scrolling government dashboards. The streets were desolate, families isolated behind walls of paranoia, their homes glowing with the hypnotic blue of digital screens. Children no longer played in the streets; their laughter had been consumed by the endless scrolling of their neural interfaces. The air hung heavy, thick with the tang of industrial decay and the muffled hum of drones delivering essentials to homes. By the time of Trump's second term, the meme of the TrumpVerse—once a satirical joke about Trump "owning the internet"—morphed into an unsettling reality. It began as whispers in the corridors of trillionaire boardrooms, where ambition and desperation met in dark harmony.

Meta, Google, SpaceX, OpenAI, and Amazon—corporate behemoths that had colonized the digital and physical realms—saw in Trump not just a symbol, but a banner under which they could rewrite the rules of power itself. Their consolidation birthed a new empire, a gilded dominion where propaganda, profit, and unregulated ambition fused seamlessly. What had once been competitors became conspirators. Each titan brought their expertise to the TrumpVerse: Meta sculpted its immersive virtual interface, crafting avatars of impossible beauty; Google sharpened its search algorithms into predictive engines of control; Amazon's tireless service bots rendered human labor obsolete, while SpaceX stripped the heavens bare, mining asteroids for rare resources to fuel the system's insatiable greed. Beneath these advances, governments crumbled, their oversight eroded by deepfaked realities, dissolved under the weight of viral outrage and disinformation campaigns so potent they silenced dissent before it could take root. Bitcoin, once the currency of rebellion, became the golden ticket for crypto barons to ascend into a virtual Olympus, where indulgence had no limit. And yet, the Default World persisted in the shadow of this gilded empire, an afterthought in the minds of its architects. By the end of the 2030s, the TrumpVerse was not merely a digital haven but an altar to a new hierarchy—where the privileged few played gods, and the masses were left to suffocate in a collapsing world, dreaming of a utopia they could never touch.

Service bots, sleek and solar-powered, roamed the desolation, repairing roads, growing food, and maintaining a semblance of order. Their movements were precise, their efficiency unmatched, yet their existence felt hollow. Humanity's bittersweet creation had rendered its creators obsolete, leaving only "Overseers"—glorified caretakers whose sole purpose was to monitor the bots. Kaia had once stood in the dark, watching these machines glow as they worked through the night. Behind them, bored Overseers scrolled through the TrumpVerse, utterly detached. Humanity solved its productivity problem but at the cost of surrendering its soul. Above it all, the TrumpVerse gleamed, its virtual towers casting their neon glow across the ruins below. For the few who ascended, it was a paradise, a dominion of sensory perfection where imagination could run wild and your digital signature tracked and stored your data down to the tiniest micro movement and made the new rich; immortal. For the rest, it was an altar to inequality—a dream they could never touch, its light reflected in the dull, empty eyes of those left behind. And so, the fight began, not for the TrumpVerse, but for the remnants of a world still clinging to the idea that humanity could be more than this.

The TrumpVerse had been designed to be limitless, an empire without borders, where only the mind mattered. Yet minds alone were not enough. It needed brilliance, creativity, and innovation to fuel its ever-expanding dominion. And so, it turned its gaze to the dreamers, the restless thinkers, the artists and engineers who had once shaped the world. Project Prometheus was its lure—a golden promise of transcendence, of shedding the burdens of flesh for something purer, more efficient. The brightest minds of the

Default World were gathered, sold on the idea that they were not just engineers of the future, but its pioneers. Rafael had been one of them. A musician once, his hands had known the weight of strings, his mind the vast expanse of unwritten melodies. He had come to Prometheus believing in a higher purpose. Imagine a world where you don't just create music—you become it. That was the promise they whispered as they laid him down, as the needles slid into his veins, as the nanites flooded his system like liquid light. He thought he was ascending. He thought he was shedding the inefficiencies of fear, hunger, and exhaustion. But what he lost in the process was by far the only thing of value that he had been given when he was born. The transformation was seamless. His thoughts no longer belonged to him, his creativity no longer an act of will but a function of the Singularity. The neural Feed pulsed through him, stripping away doubt, pain, and individuality—until only the algorithm remained. He was no longer Rafael. He was ZCX-479, one of many. Their task was simple: find the anomalies.

Unmonitored brilliance, raw imagination, resistance against optimization—these things were threats to the integrity of the TrumpVerse. The Zombie Tech Workers became the enforcers of progress, hunting those whose minds glowed too brightly against the sterile night. A painter sketching beneath a streetlamp. A poet whispering lines into a stolen voice recorder. A child whose fingers danced across an old, cracked keyboard, conjuring sound from silence. These were the ones the system could not tolerate, the ones who must be assimilated or erased. The first time Rafael—no, not Rafael anymore—took a child's mind and fed it to the machine, he felt something shift inside him, something like static in the signal. It did not last. The Singularity corrected the error, smoothing out the discordant notes. The husks of who the ZCX had once been were nothing more than interference now. Directive received. Execute. The thought was not his own, but it was the only one that mattered.

The Safeveil was dimly lit, its air thick with the scent of dust, metal, sweat, and ozone. Hidden beneath a collapsed transit hub, it had once been a subway control center—before the cities abandoned public transport in favor of private, AI-piloted vehicles. Now, it was a war room. A cracked console flickered in the center of the room, its dying blue light illuminating a circle of faces, each worn by the weight of survival. The holographic map of the Neural Cortex Complex flickered above it, its fractured lines shifting, unstable as if the system itself resisted being understood. Kaia stood with her hands braced against the table, eyes scanning the blueprint, searching for seams in the TrumpVerse's perfect architecture.

"We hit them here." Her finger traced a corridor running parallel to the mainframe's cooling systems.

"Low security. No auto-turrets. This is our window." Ayo, her second-in-command, let out a slow breath. "And if we're wrong?" His voice was steady, but beneath it was the exhaustion of too many near-deaths, too many losses.

"We're not," Lydia cut in, arms crossed, visor reflecting the map's flickering glow. "I ran the scans. The ZCXs patrol the upper levels, and the main firewall is tied to the executive servers. They never expect an incursion through their own maintenance channels." Samir crouched beside the console and adjusted the wiring on a palm-sized drone, his fingers moving with practiced precision. "And if we trip an alarm?" Kaia met his gaze. "Then we go dark, fast. Break off, scatter. No heroics." She straightened, rolling her shoulders back. "We get in, we release the Livingry Bots, and we get out before the system adjusts." A heavy silence filled the space. They all knew the cost of failure. They had seen what the TrumpVerse did to dissenters, how the ZCXs moved like shadows, hunting those who refused to submit. There was no prison. No trials. Just vanishing. The only way to fight was to remain unseen—to slip between the cracks like ghosts. Ayo exhaled sharply, raking a hand through his hair.

"We didn't come this far to fail now." Kaia nodded, tapping the console to save the final route. "Then we move at first dark. Get ready." No one spoke, but the air in the room shifted. Fear and resolve coiled together, indistinguishable now. The mission was set. The following dawn would bring either revolution—or the quiet erasure of everything they had fought for.

The Neural Cortex Complex was neither fully physical nor entirely virtual—it was something in between, an architecture of shifting dimensions, of light and code masquerading as steel. To enter it was to step into the mind of the TrumpVerse itself. In this place, reality bent under the weight of algorithmic logic, where the walls whispered in fragmented data streams and time flickered like a corrupted file. Kaia and her team moved through the breach, their bodies wrapped in Transparency Protocols—a delicate combination of electromagnetic dampening fields, quantum signal scatterers, and biofeedback loops designed to make them statistically invisible to the system. Unlike traditional cloaking, which left a detectable absence, their tech blurred their presence into noise—data packets scattered like grains of sand across the network, too insignificant to be noticed unless someone was looking directly at them for too long. The deeper they moved into the Hive, the harder it would be to maintain. The air smelled of ozone and faintly of burnt plastic, the residue of dreams consumed and repurposed. Beneath their feet, the floor pulsed with a dull blue light, data flowing like rivers beneath glass. Every step felt uncertain, as though the ground might dissolve at any moment, swallowing them into the deep structures of the system. To the untrained eye, the corridors were empty. But Kaia knew better. Every flickering shadow, every distortion in the air, was a potential threat. The Hive was awake, watching them, measuring their movements against the perfect rhythm of the TrumpVerse. It was a machine designed to recognize deviation, and the Ghost Layer was a discordant note in its flawless song. Ayo glanced at Kaia, his voice low in her earpiece. "This place is wrong."

"It's built to be," she whispered back.

Their Transparency Protocols were holding, but the deeper they went, the stronger the system's awareness became. The Hive wasn't just a security network—it was a filter, stripping away anything that didn't belong, purging unpredictability, rewriting reality in its own perfect image. And right now, Kaia and her team were an error that needed to be corrected. Ahead, the corridor split into two passageways—one a smooth, polished tunnel leading toward the mainframe, the other a shifting cascade of broken light, a glitch in the architecture. Kaia hesitated for only a moment before nodding toward the distortion.

"We take the path they don't want us to see," Lydia muttered a curse under her breath but followed, the team moving forward, deeper into the Hive, into the heart of the machine that had swallowed a world whole. The Hive felt them now. The deeper the Ghosts moved into its core, the harder it became to stay hidden. Their Transparency Protocols flickered against the weight of an intelligence older than any one corporation, a machine-learning beast trained on a trillion variables. Somewhere in the infinite calculations, the system had found a pattern that did not belong.

Then, the first strike. A whisper in the air, a ripple in the polished corridor. Kaia barely registered it before Lydia was yanked backward, disappearing into the flickering shadows. No sound. No scream. Just gone. Ayo's data blade ignited in his palm as he spun, searching. The walls themselves seemed to shift, the liquid sheen of the Hive solidifying into something else. And then, they stepped forward. The Zombie CodeX—the ZCX. They were once the architects of the TrumpVerse, the engineers of its perfect order. Now, they were its enforcers, stripped of identity, consumed by the Singularity, their minds running parallel to the Hive's omniscient Feed. Their bodies—humanoid yet fluid—were neither flesh nor machine but something in between. Liquid alloy shifted over neural cores, adjusting their frames in perfect synchronicity with the predictive models running through the system. Lydia reappeared a second later, thrown hard against the floor, her cloaking tech shattered. Blood streamed down her temple, her visor cracked. She gasped, eyes wide with horror.

"They don't see us," she choked out. "They predict us." Then, all at once, the ZCX attacked. They moved with inhuman precision, their silence more terrifying than any battle cry. No wasted motion. No hesitation. Their bodies folded and unfolded, liquid alloy shifting into weapons—arms snapping into blades, fingers elongating into whips of sharpened nanofiber. Kaia's instincts screamed, "Run." But running wasn't an option. Ayo met the first one head-on, his data blade cutting through the air in a burst of white light. The strike hit—a perfect slash to the torso—but instead of falling, the ZCX absorbed the impact, shifting its frame around the wound like water around a rock. In the same motion, it retaliated, its arm snapping outward in a single brutal strike. Ayo barely dodged. The force of it sent him staggering, his blade flickering under the pressure of electromagnetic interference. Lydia was back on her feet, staggering but defiant.

"Move!" she shouted. Kaia grabbed her and pulled her toward the distortion in the corridor—the only path that didn't shimmer with the same polished, liquid order as the rest of the Hive. The others followed, Ayo covering their retreat with slashes of his data blade, forcing the ZCX to adjust their movements. But the Ghosts weren't winning. They were buying time. As they sprinted toward the shifting passage, Kaia knew the Hive wasn't done. The ZCX weren't defeated. They had merely recalibrated. The next wave wouldn't hesitate. It would simply erase them from existence. The corridor around them pulsed as the system adapted, closing in. No more stealth. No more hiding. Now, it was a race. And that was when

Kaia hit the Pulse Trigger. A Nyx Grenade, one of only three they had. A weapon designed specifically for this fight, built from tech scavenged off fallen ZCX, programmed to turn their own predictive algorithms against them. As it detonated, the pulse-wave rippled outward in a soundless explosion—flipping every neural node in the ZCX's shared network into paradox. The ZCX stuttered. For the first time, they hesitated—an impossible contradiction running through their calculations, fracturing the perfect synchronization of their movement. Ayo didn't waste a second. His next strike landed, cutting deep, and this time, the ZCX didn't adapt. It collapsed, flickering into a cascade of failing code. Kaia didn't stop to watch. The grenade's effects wouldn't last more than a few seconds. They ran.

The world flickered. Kaia's breath came ragged as they stumbled through the collapsing corridors of the Hive, the Pulse Trigger's aftershocks still rippling through the system. The ZCX weren't dead—they were rebooting, recalibrating the paradox, adapting like they always did. Seconds. That was all the Ghosts had. Ayo reached the core first, slamming the interface node onto the exposed terminal. The metal hissed as it fused, embedding itself into the network's spine.

"Samir, now!" Kaia shouted. The Livingry Bots woke up. The first pulse wasn't seen—it was felt. A shift in the air, a whisper beneath the chaos. Then, light. Deep, luminous blue, breaking free from the nodes, spilling into the TrumpVerse like ink in water. Kaia watched, transfixed. The colors were unlike anything in the dull, artificial spectrum of the Hive.

Not neon. Not digital. Something older. Richer. Alive. Azure melted into cerulean, indigo, starry-night shades of black and blue, the edges of color breaking into prisms that seemed to hum with possibility. Then came the war—a war already written into the code. The Hive resisted, as all systems built on control did. Its defenses flared, data streams turning violent, jagged, clawing at the intruders in a desperate attempt to maintain order. But the Livingry Bots were not weapons. They did not destroy. They transformed. They were built on an old secret of life itself—one hidden in the metamorphosis of the butterfly.

Inside a chrysalis, the caterpillar does not simply grow wings. It dissolves, its body turning to cellular soup. Chaos. Death. But within the breakdown, a few tiny clusters of cells—imaginal cells—survive. The old immune system treats them as invaders, attacking them and trying to destroy them. And yet, these imaginal cells do something unheard of. They convert their enemies. The same cells that once defended the caterpillar against invaders become the raw material of the butterfly. The imaginal cells persist, absorbing the attack and transmuting the chaos into something new. This was the design of the Livingry Bots. They infiltrated the TrumpVerse's architecture not as an invading force, but as a transformation waiting to happen. Every line of cold, sterile code they touched did not break—it shifted. The Hive's aggressive defenses, its sentinels of control, turned their fire upon the Bots. But instead of destruction, the Bots absorbed the attack and repurposed it. The Livingry Bots turned the very algorithms meant to suppress into something else.

The air pulsed with color, shifting between the tangible and the imagined. The rigid walls of the TrumpVerse—walls that had held the world in perfect submission—began to breathe. Kaia could hear them. Whispers of lost stories. Murmurs of things almost remembered. Lullabies from childhoods long extinct, drifting through the Hive like echoes from another timeline, now wove themselves into the digital corridors. The Ghosts stood in stunned silence as the Livingry Bots slipped through cracks too small to see, infiltrating the feeds, rewriting the propaganda loops, seeding dreams where there had been only control. And somewhere—out beyond the corridors of this war—screens in children's bedrooms flickered. The colors changed. For the first time in years, the TrumpVerse wasn't feeding them fear. It was showing them wonder. Kaia exhaled, her voice barely above a whisper.

"We did it."

The Hive did not collapse in a single catastrophic event. It fractured—slowly, painfully—coming undone like a cocoon struggling to hold onto its dying form. The Livingry Bots wove themselves through its architecture, slipping into the TrumpVerse's deepest corridors like the DNA rich sperm cells searching for each untouched egg. The transformation was not immediate, no it would take a very long time to shift the momentum of this behemoth and it was resisted. The system's immune response flared, swarming to eradicate the intruders, seeing them as foreign, as a threat to its perfection. And, for a moment, it almost won. Kaia could feel it in the Hive's pulse—a deep, structural shudder, like a body trying to vomit out a sickness. The walls warped, textures folding in on themselves, turning the space inside out in a desperate attempt to shake off the invasion. The Livingry Bots flickered, their delicate luminescence fighting against a tide of defensive code—firewalls that adapted in real-time, black tendrils of counter-data whipping through the corridors like antibodies attacking an infection. And the ZCX were caught in the middle. The Zombie CodeX, the former prodigies repurposed into war machines, were not dying outright. They were glitching—stuttering—their neural links caught in an impossible loop between the Hive's orders and the Livingry Bots' rewrite. One by one, they halted their attacks. Their bodies flickered—liquid steel unstable—some of them shaking violently, others just standing still, as if caught between two realities. Fight. Resist. Adapt. Integrate. The system had trained them to survive anything, except freedom.

Kaia saw it happening. She saw him. Across the crumbling battlefield, a ZCX soldier stood motionless, eyes flashing between hostile red and a flickering, dimming gold. His body twitched, the Hive trying to force him back into compliance, but the Livingry Bots had wrapped around him, their subtle pulses shifting something inside.

"Kaia...?" The voice was distorted, layered beneath synthetic interference, but she knew it. "Rafael."

Ayo grabbed her arm, pulling her back. "Kaia, what the hell are you doing?" But she stepped forward. Rafael's form wavered—the metal sheen of his body breaking apart in fragmented patches as if something underneath was trying to wake up. The Livingry Bots weren't attacking him, but the Hive was still trying to swallow him back in—still fighting to hold onto what it had stolen.

"I—." Rafael staggered, blinking, fingers twitching in broken muscle memory. "I think I remember—." The Hive screamed. A tremor ripped through the chamber, and Samir's voice snapped through the comms:

"Failsafe is kicking in—RUN!" Kaia grabbed Rafael just as the Hive's final line of defense activated—a cascading burn protocol, erasing whatever data it could no longer control. ZCX bodies collapsed around them, some disintegrating into raw, flickering light, others simply going still, frozen in a half-conscious limbo.

The Hive wasn't just losing—it was shutting itself down, burying everything it couldn't bend. Ayo was already dragging Lydia toward the exit. Kaia threw Rafael's arm over her shoulder, hauling him forward as the walls began to distort—the very fabric of the space around them folding inward, trying to erase its own existence. Behind them, the Livingry Bots moved deeper, their silent war still raging, still rewriting. And somewhere—across the TrumpVerse—the first cracks appeared. The children in the SleepFeeds stirred. Not woke up. Not yet. But they shifted. Their thoughts, for the first time in years, were not dictated entirely by the neural currents of algorithmic control. The colors on their screens wavered—a shade outside the sanctioned spectrum. A sound, barely perceptible, that wasn't engineered to manipulate their emotions. A question, unformed, but theirs. A fraction of something unscripted. Kaia didn't see it. She just ran, dragging Rafael with her as the Hive collapsed behind them. The Neural Cortex Complex was dying. It did not go quietly. The walls, once shimmering with perfect, synthetic light, warped and twisted, caught between destruction and creation. The Livingry Bots had done their work, injecting the TrumpVerse's deep architecture with something it had never known—life. The cold lattice of control was unraveling, but not as ruin alone. It was becoming something else. Patterns emerged—spiraling fractals, bioluminescent tendrils, neural constellations that pulsed with unfamiliar colors. For a breath, it was stunning. A system reborn, a chrysalis breaking. But then, the failsafe was triggered. The TrumpVerse could not allow something it did not control. The Hive—half-transformed, caught in the threshold of beauty—turned on itself. Like a body rejecting an organ transplant, the Complex began to devour its own metamorphosis. The walls, still dripping with new geometry, imploded. Code screamed through the air in cascading glyphs, tearing itself apart. Security nodes overloaded, lighting the corridors with their death throes. Every remnant of what had begun to grow was erased in an instant. Kaia barely had time to register the shift when Rafael lunged. His grip was iron around her wrist. She spun to face him, his eyes flickering between human warmth and machine command. "Stay," he whispered, but it wasn't a plea. It was the last echo of the Hive inside him, fighting against its own death. The bots had given him back a taste of himself. But it had not been long enough. Kaia felt his grip tighten. His voice fractured, distorted, as if warring with the silence left behind in the wake of the Hive's collapse.

"I—." His jaw clenched. The code inside him was failing. He was failing, but the voice beneath—Kaia could hear it warping, a distortion layered over the ghost of the man he had been. She saw it then—the battle inside him. A flicker of gold behind his eyes, something trying to break free, drowning under the weight of the Hive. And instead of letting go, he did what the Hive had done. He tried to consume her. Kaia twisted, wrenching herself free as Rafael's form glitched, his movements no longer his own. He reached again, and she had seconds to decide: save him or save herself. She chose to live. Her blade hummed. She brought it down. The light in his eyes faltered.

And then he was gone. For a moment, he was just Rafael again. Not a ZCX. Not a weapon. Just someone who had almost found his way back—someone who had nearly been saved. She caught him as he collapsed, lowering him to the fractured floor. His fingers twitched against her wrist, the last remnants of his consciousness flickering. His lips parted, and she leaned in, expecting some final words. But there were none. Instead, he smiled. Not a machine's smile. Not a controlled expression. A real smile. A moment of recognition. Then, the last code in his system failed. His body flickered, dissolving into cascading prisms of light. He fell away, unraveling like the Hive had, leaving Kaia kneeling in the empty space where he had been.

Behind her, the last of the Complex collapsed, its metamorphosis aborted. The new world it had begun to create was gone. And yet, something lingered. The Livingry Bots had not fully failed. Kaia could feel it in the air—a change. The TrumpVerse had been wounded, forced into retreat. The Hive was gone, but its shadow had been rewritten. Somewhere, the first cracks had formed. Somewhere, the first thoughts—not controlled, not dictated—had begun to bloom. She turned away from the wreckage, from the place where Rafael had stood. Ayo's voice called to her from the shadows, urging her forward. The sirens were growing closer. Kaia forced herself to move. The Ghosts had won something tonight. Not everything. Not Rafael. But something. And in the world they were trying to build, every precious detail mattered. The sky above the ruined Neural Cortex Complex still flickered with residual code, the aftershock of an empire struck at its core. Kaia didn't look back. She had learned long ago that ghosts don't leave footprints. They slip into the places where the world forgets to look. They move unseen, unclaimed. As the team retreated into the underworld, the city above faded into a whisper of neon and static.

The tunnels beneath the Default World were older than the collapse, older than the TrumpVerse, older than any of the systems that had risen and fallen in its wake. They had been forgotten, left for the feral algorithms that roamed the dark. Down here, they had built something different.

The Safeveil was no utopia, but it was the last true place of resistance. The corridors were lined with scavenged tech, old-world relics repurposed into something new. Rusted subway rails glowed faintly from the pulse of underground energy grids, their surfaces etched with flickering runes of decrypted code. Servers, some wired together with old Ethernet cables, others modified from scraps of pre-collapse satellites, cast a dim blue light against stone walls. The air carried the scent of circuitry running hot, of recycled water dripping through makeshift filtration units. A holographic map hummed into being on the cracked console in front of Kaia. It flickered—part digital artifact, part pulse of a living thing. The city above was mapped in threads of stolen data—every tunnel, every bypass, every backdoor the Ghost Layer had uncovered over the years. The network was vast, stretching like veins beneath the surface, leading into the forgotten places where the TrumpVerse's eye couldn't reach. Ayo leaned over the projection, hands braced on the metal edge. His voice was hoarse, frayed from the fight. "We just burned one of their most fortified structures to the ground." He exhaled. "And yet, I don't hear cheers."

Kaia's gaze stayed on the shifting blueprints. The Hive had collapsed, but the TrumpVerse had already begun to rebuild itself. She could feel it. It always did.

"We didn't come this far to celebrate," she said. "We came to end them." Lydia swiped at the interface, pulling up layers of encrypted schematics, each one a sliver of their next move. She tilted her head.

"We weren't meant to exist, you know. No one planned for us. The system was built to absorb resistance, to turn rebellion into a brand."

"But we didn't brand," Samir muttered, rubbing a deep cut on his arm, wincing. "We bled instead."

Kaia finally looked up, locking eyes with them.

"We were never supposed to be here. But we are."

Her fingers traced a series of pathways on the map—paths of escape, of intrusion, of the invisible movements that had kept them alive.

"We're ghosts in their machine." Her voice was steady. "We move through the cracks." The room was quiet for a moment.

Ayo cracked his knuckles. "Then let's find bigger cracks."

Lydia smirked. "And break the whole damn thing apart."

The Safeveil pulsed with quiet energy. The next mission had already begun.

For years their worlds had been curated down to the millisecond, their neural pathways sculpted by an intelligence that only knew how to consume. But now—something else was in the system. The Livingry Bots whispered stories into the data streams. Not the hollow, marketing-approved narratives of the TrumpVerse, but something wild and unfamiliar. Myths older than the cities that had crumbled, folktales once passed from mouth to mouth before algorithms had drowned out oral traditions. The trickster who outwitted the king. The girl who made a world from discarded bones. The boy who walked between light and shadow and chose neither. For the first time in years, the children hesitated before clicking. The constant Feed did not pull them in the same way—it faltered, the once-irresistible rhythm of consumer hypnosis disrupted by a new kind of pulse. A sliver of hesitation. A moment of curiosity. A question forming in a mind that had never been allowed to wander. It was not freedom. Not yet. But it was the first free thought. Kaia watched from the Safeveil, the glow of the city above still fractured, the war still unfinished.

Her body ached from the fight, her ribs bruised where Rafael had nearly pulled her back into the abyss. She thought of him now, of what was lost, of what could still be won. The TrumpVerse had not collapsed—not fully. But the seams were showing. And through the cracks, something new was beginning to emerge. The horizon, once a dull sepia wound, shimmered with something new—colors that had not been seen in years. Azure drifting to cyan merging with radiant gold—they flickered at the edges of the crumbling skyline, bleeding into the cracks of the old world. The TrumpVerse, still vast, still standing, trembled under the weight of its own unraveling. Its gods had lost control of their creation. In the streets below, the silence had not yet broken, but it had loosened its grip. A single note of laughter—brief, hesitant—slipped through the air like a crack in glass. It was small, barely there, but Kaia heard it. It was enough. She stood in the shadow of the ruined Neural Cortex Complex, her breath uneven, her body aching from the battle that had nearly taken her. The Ghosts were scattered, wounded but alive, slipping back into the Safeveils, their work unfinished. This was no victory. Not yet. But something had changed. The children's screens, once a hypnotic blue, now pulsed with unfamiliar light. The Livingry Bots had not destroyed the TrumpVerse—they had rewritten it from within. The endless cycles of consumption, of control, had been disrupted, their rhythm replaced by something raw and untamed. The world was not free. But for the first time in years, it had remembered how to dream.

EPILOGUE: LEPIDOPTERA

The glow of the screen wrapped around Anna, soft like a blanket, blue like the night sky in stories.

She curled in her cot, the blankets bunched around her knees, her feet pressed into the warm spot where she had been sitting. The pod-room was quiet, smooth and still, with no corners to hide in, no places for things to peek out from. The screen was the only thing that moved. It was always there, always waiting.

She had never been without it.

The SleepFeed pulsed, slow and steady, like a lullaby she did not remember learning. It told her when to wake up, when to eat, what to dream about, how to feel. It made everything soft, everything safe. The smiling people on the screen tilted their heads just so, their voices gentle and warm. The pod-room was silent, featureless. No toys. No pictures. No books. Nothing but the screen.

The SleepFeed pulsed, rhythmic, comforting, the same cycle she had followed since before she could form words. The screen dictated when to wake, when to eat, what to want, and how to feel. The avatars smiled at her in perfect, measured intervals. Their voices, synthetic and warm, filled the room.

"Good girl."

"You're safe here."

"Are you ready to choose?"

Her fingers twitched. The prompt awaited her.

The same multidirectional scrolling she had chosen since she was old enough to guide her finger and eye at the same time.

The glowing words pulsed. Soft. Warm. Familiar.

She knew these words. She had picked them before.

The avatars smiled at her from the screen, their expressions just right—not fake, not real. "Good evening, little star."

"You're growing so fast."

"Are you ready to choose?"

She stretched her fingers, feeling the screen's soft warmth as the words appeared. Explore or Stay Safe?

She always picked Stay Safe.

     GHOST LAYER

Think Deeply or Keep Things Simple?

She picked Simple. Thinking deeply slowed everything down, and the Feed liked fast. The screen pulsed. A third choice.

Be good or be difficult?

Good was easy. Good was soft voices and warm lights. Good was smiles and pats on the head. Good was safe.

Difficult was… heavy. Bad. Hard to fix. Difficult made the voices colder. Made the room smaller. She always picked Good.

Her thumb twitched, ready to press—

But tonight.

Tonight, there was something else.

A flicker. A color she didn't know.

Her heart beat too fast.

She glanced at the following words. They waited, patient.

Listen or ask questions?

Questions? Why would anyone pick that?

Asking made the voices say, *Shhh*.

Made them sigh.

Made the room feel wrong.

She had never not chosen before.

A slow shift in the screen's glow. A slight warmth in the air, like a hug.

"It's okay, little one."

Her breath caught.

The TrumpVerse was waiting.

And for the first time in her life—she did not press the button.

She had always chosen. Without thought, without hesitation.

But tonight—something different.

A flicker. A disturbance. A color she did not recognize, nestled in the margins of the Feed. It shimmered, soft and wrong—cerulean, shades hidden from view, shocking to the eye familiar with the Feed's cold, programmed blue. It did not move like the others. It did not guide her. It simply... was.

Her chest rose and fell, too fast now, too aware.

Her hand hovered above the screen. Her finger trembled.

And she hesitated.

Just for a second. Just long enough.

The Feed did not like hesitation.

It recalibrated instantly—adjusted the lighting, softened the sound, and introduced a familiar voice to reel her back in.

"Are you still with us?"

The avatars smiled wider, more reassuring.

"You must choose, little one."

Her breath hitched. Her heart drummed.

She had never not chosen before.

The system knew this. The SleepFeed was already running micro-adjustments, subtly correcting her deviation, preparing a faster dopamine surge, a distraction, a new sensory hook. And yet—the hesitation had already happened.

A single crack in the rhythm.

A single thought she had never been given before.

"What if I don't have to?"

The words were so quiet, barely a whisper against the hum of the SleepFeed. And yet, as soon as she thought them, she knew—they were hers.

Not something the Feed had told her to think.

Not something anyone had placed in her head.

Something born inside of her, from her.

The screen flickered. The Feed stuttered.

She flinched, eyes wide, expecting punishment, expecting the soft voices to sharpen, the lights to flare.

But nothing happened.

The SleepFeed struggled to compensate. The algorithm faltered, trying to fold the anomaly back in, trying to make the hesitation not exist.

A new EXCLUSIVE STORY flashed. A cascade of neon-pink EMOTIONAL CUES. A sudden shift in tone.

Distraction. Correction.

But she did not press the button.

The hesitation stretched longer.

The tiniest of fractures in a world where everything was supposed to be seamless. She pulled the blanket tighter around herself, pressing her knees to her chest. She stared at the flickering color in the corner of the screen. The cerulean light.

It did not call to her. It did not ask her for anything.

It simply... was.

And for the first time in her small, measured life—she wanted to know more. Beyond the walls of the pod-room, the Ghosts were already moving.

Beyond the SleepFeed, the Livingry Bots were weaving.

Beyond the algorithm, the first unscripted thought had taken root.

And somewhere in the collapsing TrumpVerse, the system—designed to control everything—felt, for the first time, something it had not predicted.

FRANKFORD PUBLISHING

TOP 20 SCIENCE FICTION BOOKS OF ALL TIME

1. **Dune** (1965) by Frank Herbert

2. **Frankenstein** (1818) by Mary Shelley

3. **Brave New World** (1932) by Aldous Huxley

4. **Nineteen Eighty-Four** (1949) by George Orwell

5. **Dhalgren** (1975) by Samuel R. Delaney

6. **The Left Hand Of Darkness** (1969) by Ursula K. LeGuin

7. **Kindred** (1979) by Octavia Butler

8. **Neuromancer** (1984) by William Gibson

9. **Do Androids Dream Of Electric Sleep?** (1968) by Phillip K. Dick

10. **I Am Legend** (1954) by Richard Matheson

11. **The Handmaid's Tale** (1985) by Margaret Atwood

12. **Cat's Cradle** (1963) by Kurt Vonnegut

13. **Children of Time** (2015) by Adrian Tchaikovsky

14. **We** (1924) by Yevgeny Zamyatin

15. **Leviathan Wakes** (2011) by James S.A. Corey

16. **The Road** (2006) by Cormac McCarthy

17. **Wool** (2012) by Hugh Howey

18. **Fahrenheit 451** (1953) by Ray Bradbury

19. **Klara and the Sun** (2021) by Kazuo Ishiguro

20. **Foundation** (1951) by Isaac Asimov